THE
BOOK
OF
DESIRE

~ ANNE ~

Marilyn Kahr

The Book of Desire - Anne

Publishers note:
This book is a work of fiction. Names, characters, places and incidents are either the product of the author's imagination or are used fictitiously, and any resemblance to actual persons living or dead, events, or locales is entirely coincidental.

ISBN-13: 978-1-944916-91-6
ISBN-10: 1-944916-91-1

www.SuddenInsightPublishing.com
Indie publishing for the Indie Author

THE
BOOK
OF
DESIRE

~ ANNE ~

CHAPTER 1

Anne hesitated on the sidewalk before going in. She could see Raina through the window, already sitting at a table. Her friend was smiling, as usual; and glowing with it, as usual. Raina was talking to the waiter, a young man who showed no sign of having anything better to do. They were both nodding while she spoke, him oblivious to his customers and her similarly oblivious to the other young man watching the exchange.

Anne pulled the door open, her eyes still on her friend. She shifted her attention between the exchange and its spectator as she approached the table. He was handsome, and not in a Maysville kind of way. He took as long to notice her as Raina did. As Anne pulled out a chair, Raina beamed at her and the handsome stranger looked away.

"Hi sweetie!" Raina exclaimed.

Raina launched to her feet before Anne could sit. The waiter was forgotten, although he still stood there smiling. Raina brushed past him to embrace Anne. The embrace was as graceful and easy for Raina as it was awkward and difficult for Anne. She leaned over the table, feeling its hard edge digging painfully into her thigh as her friend hugged her tighter.

Over Raina's shoulder, Anne saw the handsome stranger watching them. He sat at a table nearby, chewing a bite of his lunch slowly. His eyes were on Raina's shapely body while her back was to him. Anne watched him watching her, noting that his eyes were blue and almond-shaped without meaning to. As his gaze drifted, he locked eyes with Anne and smiled. She blinked, looking away.

Anne moved from Raina's embrace, standing straight and looking her in the eye. She felt that familiar glow that Raina's attention seemed to impart to anyone she put her focus on. Awash in it, she forgave the waiter for standing there and the stranger for staring. They couldn't help it.

"Hey Raina," Anne smiled. She sat down. "Sorry to keep you waiting."

"Don't be silly," Raina beamed. "I just got here."

She noticed the waiter as she sat, and Raina looked up at him.

"Can we have a minute, please?" she asked sweetly.

The young man stammered a reply that contained several syllables, but no actual words. The cloud that he had just been floating on had been yanked unceremoniously out from under him. Anne's heart went out to him once more as she floated on the cloud he had just vacated. She watched with amused resignation as he gathered his thoughts and drifted off. As he moved, the handsome seated stranger came into Anne's view once more. He was looking their way, and their eyes locked again.

He winked at her.

Anne flushed and turned her attention to Raina. She was smiling, her blue eyes crinkling at the corners and lighting up at the same time. Anne let the smile wash over her, let it warm her and coax a smile from her own lips.

"I'm going to miss you," Raina said seriously, still smiling.

"It's just a week." Anne let her smile fall, then added, "I'll miss you too."

"Are you sure you won't reconsider?" Raina asked. "I could take a week off work and go with you."

Anne laughed. "To Mexico? You don't want to go to Mexico."

"Sure I do." Raina's smile turned to a frown for a split second, then morphed back into a smile. "I've heard it's beautiful down there."

"I'm not going to a resort full of tourists," Anne said with a touch of disdain. "I want to hike and explore and get a feel for the culture and the people. I want to avoid little drinks with umbrellas in them and beaches full of Americans like the plague. That's not my idea of a good time; it's yours. If you go to Mexico, it should be to one of those places."

She let the simple truth hang in the air between them for a moment, then added, "with Henry."

There was an unspoken rule between them. It might not have been the foundation of their friendship, but it made it possible for it to continue. Only Anne could bring up Henry, and she seldom did. When she did, the unwritten rule extended to give her the power to shut down the subject at any time as well. It was only fair, all things considered.

The waiter returned, and Anne was glad to feel Raina's attention shift to him. She smiled up at him, twirling a lock of dirty blonde hair around her finger as she did. Raina blinked her shining blue eyes at him twice prettily.

"Oh my gosh," Raina giggled. "We haven't even looked at the menu."

"I'll have a chicken caesar salad," Anne said abruptly. "She'll have a BLT on wheat with curly fries. I'll just have water to drink."

He wanted to ask Raina a question, clearly, but Anne had already answered them all.

"Sounds good," Raina beamed. Her eyes went to Anne again.

Anne sat up straighter as the waiter tarried in confusion once more. Finally he turned and ambled away from them.

"I worry about you, sweetie." Raina faced her across the table. Her pretty features were clouded with concern.

"Everybody does," Anne sighed. "Ever since my parents died this whole town has done nothing but worry about me."

Anne let her gaze drift, just to avoid eye contact with Raina. The handsome young stranger was still watching them between bites. Anne's dark eyes found his accidentally, and he winked at her again. She felt a flush creep up the back of her neck as she focused on her best friend once more.

They were both ready to say something, but the waiter was bringing her a glass of water. He smiled at each of them in turn as he set it in front of her. Anne looked away; Raina smiled back.

"Did either of you want some soup or salad?" he asked Raina.

She glowed at him, shaking her head.

"We'll take what we ordered," Anne murmured into her water.

The young man drifted away again.

Anne cast a dark look across the table. "Raina, you know I used to worry about losing my parents all the time when I was a kid."

"I do," Raina responded. She even glowed when she was frowning. "I know you worried about it just like any other kid does. I know you blamed yourself for it too, just like anyone who has gone through a serious loss is likely to do. I also know that there is no way you had anything to do with it. You weren't even there, sweetie."

"I imagined it," Anne whispered. "I imagined it in vivid detail, so many times. It was always a car crash, and they always both died in it. Did you do that? Did you spend hours imagining your parents dying in a specific way?"

When Raina didn't like a question or her own honest response to it, she was really quite good at answering without answering.

"It's totally normal," Raina said dismissively. "Do you really think every kid that wishes their parents dead gets their wish?"

Anne knew the territory. She had learned from experience with the school counselor, with the therapist she had talked to, and even with her best friend: they weren't interested in her true feelings, or her actual emotional state. They wanted to hear her parrot back the answers they were looking for. If she didn't, everyone would get even more worried about her.

"Why are you worried about me going to Mexico?" Anne asked quietly.

"Please!" Raina fluttered her hands helplessly over the table. "What am I not worried about? You're definitely going to get ripped off. You could get murdered. Sweetie, you could be raped."

Raina's voice fell to a terse whisper on the last word, and she looked around to see if anyone else had heard her speak it. Anne was grateful that she did; her mind was trying to get her to fire back a smarmy response. She couldn't decide whether to point out that her best friend seemed to be more okay with her being murdered than raped, or that Raina's worst-case scenario would at least involve Anne finally losing her virginity. While Raina looked around, she mercifully decided on neither. Anne's dark sense of humor seldom went over well with her friend. By the time their eyes met again, Anne had another response at the ready.

"So, are you saying that when you think of me in Mexico, you imagine me getting ripped off and murdered and raped?"

Anne didn't drop her voice to speak the dreaded word as Raina had, and Raina had to look around to make sure no one had heard once more. Before she could respond, Anne pressed on.

"Are you saying that you think imagining me in horrible scenarios is somehow going to prevent them?" Anne asked. "Isn't that at least slightly more ridiculous than me thinking that my imagining horrible scenarios about my parents caused their accident? I mean, if one were more true than the other it would probably be my theory."

Raina sighed. "I don't think I am preventing or causing anything bad by worrying about you. You know that."

She did; this was not unfamiliar territory either.

"Then why do you bother imagining me in horrible situations at all?" Anne asked, as innocently as possible.

"Everybody worries," Raina sighed.

"So if everybody decided to jump off a bridge…" Anne trailed off.

"You would apparently be the only person left alive," Raina conceded, smiling. She was so pretty when she smiled. Anne couldn't help but smile back. As adversarial as their banter may have appeared, it was always done in love. She poked at her friend one last time, playfully.

"And that's why I worry about *you*, sweetie!" Anne grinned.

The waiter brought their food then, and Anne's eyes drifted to the handsome young man at the other table. He was smiling and nodding, as if he had heard their conversation and somehow considered himself a part of it. He held his water glass up like he was toasting her and threw her another wink. It was slower this time, more salacious.

Anne felt a hot flush wash over her. She wondered what kind of scenarios he was imagining her in, and considered that they were probably more pleasant than her friend's imaginings. Anne let her mind go there for a moment. She thought of what his kisses might feel like, what they might taste of. She wondered if his touch was gentle or firm, if he would touch every place that she touched when she was alone with her own burning desire. She held his daring gaze so long that she began to feel pleasantly invaded.

Raina glanced at Anne, and then over her shoulder at the young man. She giggled as she snapped her fingers loudly right in Anne's face.

"He's cute," she said, still giggling. "Go talk to him."

Anne's hot flush turned to a cold sweat at the thought. She put her attention on her food as if it were a complicated mathematic equation. Stabbing a bit of salad and a piece of chicken, she had barely begun chewing the oversized bite when the young man was suddenly standing next to their table. He looked down at her and grinned while the food turned to cardboard in her mouth.

"Hello ladies," he said, still smiling. "I'm not from around here."

Raina giggled again. "Obviously."

Anne chewed furiously for the brief moment that he glanced at Raina.

"Would you show me around?" he asked.

He was looking at her, not Raina. Anne tried to chew the mouthful of cardboard in the most ladylike fashion she could muster.

"I'm busy," she said around the mound of tastelessness.

"Excuse me?" His smile was as beautiful as Raina's, in its own way.

"She said she'd love to," Raina piped up.

Anne glared daggers at her and swallowed the hard, wet clump.

"I'm busy," she repeated, more clearly.

She narrowed her eyes at him to show she meant it, although she didn't. He could not have possibly known that she was mentally filing away notes for later. The blue of his eyes, his wavy chestnut hair, the size and the shape of his hands…they were all hers now. Tonight she would open the files, as well as her legs; her mind would peruse the details of the files as her fingers explored the throbbing folds of her most secret flesh. But right now she stared at the handsome stranger like he was an unwelcome intruder.

Still smiling, the stranger shrugged.

"Well I hope I see you around." He was still smiling. It was still beautiful.

"My name is James, by the way," he added.

"Okay," Anne heard her voice say with a touch of irritation.

Thank you, the voice in her head said, filing away the name along with another few seconds of footage of his beautiful smile.

CHAPTER 2

It had been some time since Anne had spoken with her aunt. When she had called a few weeks ago, Clare had sounded pleasantly surprised to hear from her. When she had asked her to book travel plans to Mexico for her, Clare had surprised her in return by saying she thought it was a great idea. She had even helped with her passport. Anne didn't want to admit out loud that she might have found the whole process a daunting thing to undertake alone, but inside she knew she might not be going at all if not for Aunt Clare.

Sitting in her office, Anne felt relaxed like nowhere else in Maysville. Clare had always seemed a little too worldly for their little town, and her office was a colorful out-picturing of her inner landscape. She was the only person Anne knew that had been overseas. Her childhood was packed with memories of her aunt telling stories of the places she had been, the things she had seen. Clare had almost always travelled by herself, and there was no doubt her brave example had inspired Anne.

She looked at the array of framed posters while Clare spoke with a client on the phone. Anne watched her from the corner of her eye, wishing she could be half as confident and self-possessed as Clare. When she was finished, her aunt hung up the phone and winked at her. It made her think of the handsome young stranger in the restaurant, and the awaiting files in her mind. A deep warm current washed over her.

"Are you excited?" Clare nodded in anticipation of her answer.

Anne nodded with her. "I am. And a little scared."

Clare waved away her fears. "That will go away. Before you know it you'll be hooked on seeing how other people live all around the world. This town is too small to contain a spirit as big as yours."

Anne sighed her agreement. "Everybody keeps telling me I'm crazy for going to Mexico by myself."

Clare waved her hand again dismissively. "I went to Mexico by myself twenty years ago. I had so much fun. It's nineteen eighty-nine; Mexico is as different now as the United States is. You're as likely to get into trouble here as you are there; the only difference is, here it will be the same boring trouble with the same boring people. You'd be surprised how much fun it is to get in a little trouble in Mexico. Besides…"

She pointed at the little town newspaper on her desk. "They pulled another car from the lake last week. It's been down there for years, they say. The highway ends right there, and tourists not familiar with the terrain or the speed limits almost drive into the water every year or two. That's the kind of trouble a visitor has to worry about in Maysville. Trust me, Cabo San Lucas is a pretty quiet town. All of the tourist traps are harmless compared to driving into a lake."

They shared a laugh. Anne had forgotten that her aunt's humor could be as dark as her own. She wondered why she had let them drift apart. Backing her rolling chair up a bit, Clare opened a desk drawer and pulled out a thin stack of papers.

"This is everything you need, flight and rental car and

hotel information all filed in the order you'll need them." Clare leaned in close, reminding Anne why she had stayed out of touch so long. Aunt Clare's smiling sky eyes were far too familiar. Anne's mother had been as different from her sister as two sisters could be, but their blue eyes had been virtually identical when they smiled. Even after two years, the resemblance was almost too much. Anne felt tears gather in her own dark eyes, while that old familiar knot wound itself tighter in her belly.

"I also included some information I don't usually give other people," Clare added, still smiling at her with those eyes. "Some cool stuff to see where other tourists don't usually visit."

"Thanks, Aunt Clare." Anne smiled through her tears. It wasn't Clare's fault that she couldn't smile without looking like Anne's mom.

Clare came around the desk to give her a hug, then picked up the packet and pressed it into her hand.

"Have fun, Anne. You deserve it." There were tears in her eyes too. "And don't be a stranger when you get back."

"I won't," Anne promised. She meant it, too. Her mother had been very important to her. She resolved in that moment that it would be nice to have more reminders of her around. It would be nice to have Clare back in her life again too.

"Thanks," Anne said again. "I love you, Aunt Clare."

Anne's mother's smiling blue eyes came at her again.

"I love you too, Anne," Clare murmured.

As soon as the door swung shut behind her, Anne felt another flush of desire wash over her. Maybe it was the handsome stranger from lunch; maybe it was the scared excitement of her upcoming trip. Anne didn't know which; all she knew was that she had to get home. There was a bubble bath and an adjustable shower nozzle calling her name, along with a stack of mental files that might have her calling out a name other than 'Henry' as the gushing waves of wet became her own.

Flushing, Anne hurried to her car.

CHAPTER 3

Anne had never been on an airplane before. She had expected some kind of glamor that was not represented in the crowded smoke-filled cabin. She had assumed that choosing a non-smoking seat would mean she could breathe easy on the flight. She had assumed wrong. Anne had found her seat as quickly as possible and then shrunk into it. She was immediately uncomfortable with how comfortable the other passengers were in the alien environment.

Even before takeoff, Anne had almost shut down completely. The metal tube that had looked so big from the outside seemed so small on the inside, and people were still trickling in. Thankful that she was wedged between a window and a stranger instead of two strangers, Anne watched the luggage being loaded. She would likely just stare out the window the entire flight, and through the layover, tuning out in the unfamiliar setting. Among friends it was a harmless defense mechanism, a thin shell they could crack with a word or a smile. With strangers it was a thick metal armor with long spikes attached, and there was no reaching her in its cold protection without getting skewered.

She had the whole flight planned that way, a pleasant disengaged interlude between home and Cabo San Lucas. Anne knew she couldn't read a book; she would just stare at the jumble of letters on one page for all the long hours of the trip. Writing in her journal was even less possible; stringing together her own thoughts would be harder than reading someone else's. Besides, all the guy sitting next to her would have to do is glance over. He would suddenly know just what kind of thoughts the quiet young girl next to him entertained in the privacy of its pages.

Now, that would be an awkward six hours.

So Anne looked out the window, despite feeling eyes on her more than once. She wasn't take-your-breath-away beautiful like Raina, but Anne was still used to feeling eyes on her. She kept hers on the tarmac until a voice over the loudspeaker demanded that she do otherwise. It wasn't until then that she realized why she kept feeling someone watching.

A young man sat in the same row as her, just across the aisle. He leaned halfway into the open space between banks of seats, looking right at her. Everyone else faced forward; he faced sideways, staring directly at Anne. A half-smile curled the corner of his mouth in the most alluring fashion, and Anne had to fight that pull with everything she had. Keeping her face frozen and forward, Anne trained her eyes on the woman with the oxygen mask at the front of the aisle. Peripherally, all of her attention went to sizing up the handsome young man across the way.

Even sitting down, she could tell he was tall; taller than Henry even, not that it mattered. He was handsome, too, and muscled about the shoulders. He was even bigger than Henry, and probably a jock as well. Not that that mattered either. In the privacy of her mind she would admit that he was more handsome, and that it did matter; but nowhere else.

As the demonstration went from oxygen mask to seat cushion, Anne tried to sneak a glance at him. He was still facing her, but only partway. He had turned a little to watch the transition, but he turned again as she stole a look. For a long stark moment, she was looking into his dark eyes as his face broke out into a wide grin.

Finally, Anne tore her gaze away. Her heart was pounding, her armor penetrated with one searing glance. The spikes had been no use, unless that's what was poking at her brain and belly. Anne tried to look out the window again, focusing on a plane taxiing slowly down the runway.

"Hi." Anne heard the voice, but acted as though she didn't. She stared at the other plane, wishing she were on that one instead.

"Hey. Hi." He spoke again, louder.

Oh my gosh, Anne thought fervently. *Please stop, please stop, please stop.*

"Excuse me." Now the flight attendant was talking louder.

Anne glanced up at her, horrified. The woman was holding the seat cushion by her side. Her eyes were going back and forth between the young man and her, and her face was angry.

"Eyes forward," she said, her gaze on Anne's for a long melting moment. Anne wanted to sink in her chair, or look out the window, more than anything. She kept her eyes forward instead, feeling her whole body flush. Finally the woman continued, and some interminable amount of time later she finished. Anne's eyes may have been on her, but she did not register any more of the information than she had during the oxygen mask tutorial. Fortunately, there was no test afterwards.

There was, however, an even more terrifying moment to come.

"Dad," she heard a voice say, "switch me seats."

The man sitting beside her moved, and Anne's heart

began pounding once more. He shifted in his seat and looked down at her.

"Is that okay?" He smiled at her, a smile much like his son's.

No! Anne screamed inside. *No! That is so not okay!*

"That's fine," Anne heard her own voice say, betraying her.

"You can say no," the man said, smiling again.

No! Her mind screeched. *No!No!No!No!No!*

"It's fine," her voice somehow said calmly.

There was a brief bit of jostling, then the flight attendant saved her.

"Excuse me!" Her voice was even louder than before, more shrill. The woman advanced up the aisle menacingly towards father and son as they stood.

"Excuse me!" she said again. "Please stay seated until the aircraft is in the air and the pilot has turned off the 'fasten seatbelt' sign. Like I said."

The man settled in, apologizing first to the flight attendant and then to Anne. Anne mumbled a dismissive sound in response and made a show of yawning widely. Maybe she could make it look like she was sleeping by the time the pilot turned off the sign. She took off her coat and bundled it into a ball, then stuffed it between her headrest and the window. Keeping her eyes averted the whole time, she turned her body sideways and lay her head on the makeshift pillow.

There was no way she was falling asleep. This was going to be the longest six hours of her life.

CHAPTER 4

When Anne first woke up, she had no idea where she was. The lights had been dimmed in the cabin, people were asleep all around her, and her mind was foggy and disoriented. In the same moment that she realized she was awake, she realized that she had to pee. Out the window, the sky was dark; across the aisle, the young man was sleeping. Anne moved her jacket from where it was wedged and stuck it under her seat instead. She felt for her purse, just to make sure it was still there. There was no need to take it with her.

The couple that were probably the young man's parents were both sleeping, facing sideways in their seats. It was easy enough for her to slip by, and Anne was grateful that neither of them stirred as she passed. Stepping past a few more aisles, Anne turned in front of the lavatory door to face it as she grasped the handle. She gasped silently as she turned.

He was awake, and walking up the aisle behind her. He was tall, and so handsome. Anne pushed the door open as he came closer. She stepped in and let it swing shut behind her, her hand hesitating over the locking mechanism. She held her breath for a moment, thinking of stories she had heard and fantasies she had had. He must be out there by now, choosing between the other bathroom and hers. Anne couldn't hear anything over the pounding of her heart as her eyes watched the door under her hand for the most minuscule sign of movement.

Anne's hand moved forward then, and her heart began pounding harder. She watched her own hand as it grasped the handle and pulled the door inward, just a little. Still holding her breath, she let a long moment pass before she released it. Before it could swing shut and let her lock herself in with her embarrassment and shame, a hand caught it.

Smiling, looking down at her, the young man slipped into the cramped space. He let the door shut behind him and locked it.

As he turned to her, there was no room for her to be anywhere but in his arms. Pressed against him, she breathed at last. His musky scent filled her next breath as his lips pressed against hers, and Anne felt her own arms wrap around his broad shoulders. The movement felt natural and familiar, like she had embraced him a thousand times. Her breasts pressed into his hard chest as her lips opened to his, and she felt his hands clasping her buttocks. A thrill went up her spine as his big strong hands kneaded at her, each firm and gentle grasp pressing her breasts further into his chest and his tongue deeper in her mouth. His touch was playful and urgent at the same time, like his lips and his tongue were on her mouth. Anne held him still, her weight held mostly by her embrace and his strong grasping hands.

He ran one of his hands up her back, the other sliding further down. Still holding most of her weight in his hands, he leaned in closer to begin covering her neck in slow tender kisses. One of his hands was suddenly caught up in her hair, the other moving closer and closer to where her thighs came together under her pants. Anne was breathing heavy, flush with desire, when the thought hit her.

Oh my gosh, Anne's mind raced. *I'm about to lose my virginity.*

As if he had heard, his hands were suddenly still on her body. Though they continued to hold her weight, the urgent tenderness ceased abruptly. The fingers of one hand spread to hold her shoulder, where a moment ago they had been brushing her collar from the path of his lips. His kisses were finding their slow wet way from her neck to the pounding rise of her breast where they came together. The other hand was covering one buttock almost completely, his long strong fingers gripping her tight, all except one. His index finger was all the way between her legs, and a moment ago he had been using it to gently massage the flesh that was rising up to greet his touch on either side of her moist center.

The touching and the kissing stopped at her thought, and for a moment Anne was afraid she had spoken it aloud. She leaned back in his arms, watching him straighten slowly where he had bent to kiss her. Anne had been leaning over the toilet backwards, her weight suspended over it by his embrace and her feet barely touching the floor in front of it. As he straightened she did too, so they were still pressed insistently together as he looked down at her. His eyes were curious, his mouth turned down at the corners slightly with a frown.

"Are you okay?" He smiled, his eyes smoldering. He somehow glanced around the tight quarters without looking away from her. "Is this okay?"

Anne moved into him, pressing her breasts into his chest and her throbbing mound against his finger. She nodded, not trusting her voice.

"Are you sure?" He still had his hands on her, but they only held her.

Anne nodded again, then let her hands fall from his

shoulders. She trailed her fingers lightly along each of his muscled arms, tracing the long lines of sinew and noting the hard soft feel of his skin under her touch. She dropped her hands to her waist and grasped the thin cotton bottom of her blouse. In one slow movement, she lifted the material over her head and off one arm. She let the other arm fall to her side, and the blouse drop to the floor. He had to let her go partway through, and he leaned back against the door to watch with wide hungry eyes as she unclipped her bra and let it fall to the floor as well. He was waiting to see if she would continue, so she did.

Her heart pounding and her eyes on his, Anne unbuttoned her capri pants while she slipped off her sandals. Somehow she slipped out of them in the cramped space without taking a spill, and suddenly she was standing there in her underwear with a fully clothed stranger. He continued to lean against the door and watch, his gaze going from her eyes to her panties and back again. Anne thought for a moment of the carefully trimmed landing strip she had cultivated since high school. She thought of how in all the time she had maintained it, a total of zero people had ever seen it.

Taking a breath, Anne slid her panties over her hips. She felt them drift past her knees to puddle at her feet. She stepped out of them and looked up at him, lifting her arms to encircle his broad shoulders once more.

Those big hands were on her body again at last, stronger than before as he grasped her buttocks and pulled her nearly off the floor. She felt the skin of his arms and his hands on her, the soft scratchy feel of his face on her breasts all around each wet kiss. Her breasts were against his shirt, and it felt rough and cold next to the soft warmth of the other contact. She felt her weight being slowly lowered to the floor again, and Anne was glad when he straightened once more to lift his own shirt over his head. She watched him as shamelessly as he had watched her, letting her eyes go wide at the sight of his broad chest and muscled abdomen as he had let his go wide at the sight of her breasts. Kneeling before her, he raised his eyes and smiled at her.

Anne watched as he reached behind her with the t-shirt in his hand. Looking back over her naked shoulder, she saw him lay the fabric carefully flat on the lid of the toilet seat. His hands grasped her thighs above her knees, his long fingers nearly encircling each leg. Wordlessly, his breath on her belly and gently coaxing fingers encouraged her to sit.

Bending her knees, Anne felt his shirt under her skin and the cold lid of the toilet under that. His hands were still encircling her thighs, and he lifted one of her legs over his shoulder and then the other while he dipped lower into his kneeling position. Anne realized what he was doing just as her head hit the wall and his breath hit her wet hunger. One of his hands slid up her back, to support her weight and caress her drifting hair. The other was gently massaging her belly and the rise of her mound, opening her over and over to his hot drifting breaths as his kisses tickled her thighs.

His tender kisses turned to feathered licks as his face came closer to her glistening wetness. She felt his tongue on her all around the building fire, making her slick everywhere that she was not already wet with desire. It was almost too much, his hand on her belly and breasts while his breathy licking took her from hot and moist to pleasantly overwhelming swampy inferno. Anne felt like she might laugh or cry, or both; instead she leaned back further into his hand and the wall and spread her legs wider over his broad shoulders.

His mouth found her fire then, and suddenly it was too much. Anne felt his mouth encompass her, felt his gentle feathered tongue touch the sensitive folds of her moist flesh. The waves of pleasure that had been washing over her became a tsunami of sensation, and she tumbled around helplessly inside the intensity of her own pleasure while her flavor flooded his mouth. Now she was going to laugh, or cry; or at least cry out. She gasped instead, and spoke.

"Inside me," Anne whispered intensely. "I want you inside me."

He straightened before her slowly, and Anne came back to herself just enough to watch him work himself free of his jeans. He was hard, and out, and moving towards her…she didn't know if it was big or not, it was the first one she had ever seen in real life; it certainly looked big, bigger than the tiny hole that she had never even put a finger in…then he was inside her, just a little bit…then Anne did cry out, just a little bit.

It was more pleasure than pain, but it was the shocking pain of a pleasurable new sensation. Anne felt him inside her, as gentle there as he had been with his tongue and his touches. He moved around inside of her, the little bit that he had given her massaging her in a way that started a whole new series of tingling waves that came to wash her away once more. She watched the rest of him, saw the pulsing throb along the length of him that she could feel pounding like a heartbeat inside her.

Anne let a low moan escape her lips. She got one hand under her and lifted her hips to press herself closer to him. He rose to meet her, and their bodies came together again as the length of him moved inside her. Anne was trembling, her whole body suspended in his arms and by their sweet togetherness. She looked down, and couldn't see where he ended and she began. They were one body together, and she was filled up and held close by their intimate union. It was too much again, but it was a too much she couldn't get enough of. Anne moved her hips against his while she gasped and grasped at his hair. She pulled his head down to hers, kissing his lips and tasting her own wet desire on them.

She had brought herself pleasure plenty of times in the past, the way she had heard most girls did. Anne's fingers and an adjustable shower head had helped her maintain her sanity since puberty had ushered her into a hot and wet new world what seemed like lifetimes ago. But this was not like that; this was a rushing burning wave building deep inside her. It rumbled in her depths more than it lapped at her shores, and Anne felt an explosion building inside of her that she feared may push him right back out of her.

A low breathy whimper dripped from her lips, then another. Anne watched him moving in and out of her in time with the sounds, and she was helpless to stop them. She heard her own voice sound to the rhythm of his glistening throbbing movement, felt the depths of her lifetimes of desire stir in the undertow. Anne threw her head back, not noticing or caring that it hit the hard wall. She tasted him on her lips, and herself. She felt every cell of her body begin to tingle with the intensity of whatever it was building up to, and her series of quiet whimpers became one long soft moan that changed pitch with the motion of him moving his throbbing length in and out of her.

Anne lost herself completely there in the hot rushing waves as they broke faster and harder, and washed over her inside and out.

CHAPTER 5

Anne woke with a start, a low rolling moan caught in her throat. This time she knew where she was right away. She was sitting next to a man whose son had just invaded her dreams. Not only was he sitting next to her; he was looking at her with a kind of bemused curiosity. Glancing past him, Anne realized he wasn't the only person watching her. Every shoulder she could see from where she sat was topped by a head turned her way. Even the handsome young man she had just dreamed about had his eyes on her.

His touch had not been real. It had *felt* real; more real than her dreams had ever felt before, more real even than her life seemed sometimes. But it had not been real. Not his kiss, not his touch, not his embrace…none of it had been real. A man's mouth on her, his throbbing hardness inside her…those were still things she had never felt before. She didn't know how it could have felt so real if she had never felt it before, but it had. Anne's mind played the scene over again, and it looked more like a memory than a dream, even in retrospect. She pushed the memory aside, reminding herself firmly that it had not been real.

As soon as she grasped it, Anne realized that people were still looking at her. Just as her heart began to beat normally, it started racing again. Her body was flush when she woke up, and she had been moaning in her ecstasy. Had she been whimpering and moaning in her sleep, drawing everyone's attention to her before finally rousing herself? Had they heard her whisper her desires in her sleep, or her low rhythmic cries of pleasure? She was sure it was true the moment she thought it, and another flush crept over her. Anne kept her eyes on her knees and imagined the worst for several tormenting minutes.

Another realization hit her then, and gripped her just as completely. Anne really did have to pee. She clenched her thighs against the immediacy of the need, and felt her panties bunch together in a warm wet mess. She had to do more than pee; Anne needed to get cleaned up too.

She grabbed her purse this time, grateful for once that she was prepared for her body to start leaking blood at any moment. She didn't need one of the pads yet, but she could use the fresh pair of underwear stuffed in the inside pocket of her purse alongside them. They were old granny panties, but they were clean and not soaked through with her dreams.

Somehow Anne managed her way up the aisle without making eye contact with anyone. She was sure she felt them all watching her, but the only thing she saw was her feet placing themselves one before the other. She slipped into the tiny lavatory and locked the door behind her at once.

The first thing that hit her was the smell. It hadn't been that way in the dream, thankfully. It was awful, cloying and overwhelming with a perfectly rank mixture of natural and unnatural odors. Anne held her breath instinctively, but the stench had already climbed inside of her nose. She found herself wishing she had come in here before the dream; her first trip to an airplane lavatory had been a fantasy. Having a memory of the reality would surely make such fantasies impossible in the future.

Anne looked for a place to set her purse. Every surface

she could see brought a series of disgusting images from some series of strangers' bathroom activities to mind. She didn't have time to tear a thin paper seat cover to shreds and then try to piece it back together on a toilet seat whose shape barely resembled the paper's original design. She didn't have time to make a barrier for her butt on the seat, much less one for her purse on the counter. Anne slung the straps of her purse over her shoulder, lifted the toilet lid carefully with one sandaled foot, then turned and pulled her capris down past her knees. She hovered over the seat and sighed as she emptied her bladder at last.

As Anne looked around, the second thing hit her.

This disgusting-smelling space was even smaller than she had imagined it. There was no way they could have enacted her fantasy, even if they had tried. She would have surely imagined herself bent forward over the sink if she had come in here before. Looking at the smeared reflective surface, Anne wrinkled her nose thinking of her face smashed up against it.

Anne lifted one leg when she was done. She was careful to lift her foot from her sandal without brushing her heel against the waste receptacle as she bent to pull one leg of her pants off. For a frightening moment she tottered, her mind racing to choose which repulsive wall or object to touch for support. She breathed as she steadied, neither pants nor skin touching anything somehow.

Digging in her purse, balancing on one leg, Anne managed to extract her granny panties from the zippered inside pocket. She slipped her bare hovering leg into one side of the underwear and her capris, bunching them around her ankles. When her foot was snug in her sandal once more, Anne lifted the other leg and finally extricated herself from the warm wet mess. As she hovered on one leg, half of her naked while she looked for a place to put her dirty underwear, the door jiggled in place.

"It's occupied!" Anne cried, wobbling.

"The pilot has turned on the fasten seatbelt signs," a voice called through the door.

Anne frowned and stuffed the soiled cotton in her purse. Winding her other foot into the new panties and the leg of her pants, she placed her toe on her sandal and stopped teetering at last.

"Be right out!" Anne worried at the fabric bunched about her ankles. Her eyes caught her own reflection in the mirror as she did, flushed and half-naked and wobbling a bit again. She had to admit that she did look pretty sexy, all bent over. Straightening to get a better look, Anne lifted her shirt a little and watched her own slim belly come into view over her naked thighs and mound. She was so hungry down there, so hot still, for a moment she considered letting her hand drift from her stomach to the hunger that awaited. The smell assaulted her once more as another round of knocking sounded at the thin door, and Anne perished the thought.

Bending carefully, she pulled up one garment and then the other. She glanced wistfully at the sink, but had no illusions about leaving the experience any cleaner for having used it. As she opened the door, Anne felt the plane start to descend. She couldn't have been more relieved.

Anne made her way to her seat, avoiding every eye dutifully. She thought she felt the angry gaze of the flight attendant on her, then the lusty one of the young man flying with his parents; but Anne kept her eyes on the floor until she was seated, then on the window until they landed. She didn't take her lifeless stare from the transparent pane until nearly every passenger had filed past.

CHAPTER 6

Customs was not nearly the nightmare she had been warned to expect. Anne had a moment of fear when an official asked to see her purse, remembering the soiled panties she had haphazardly stuffed into it. He'd barely even glanced inside, however, tilting the open bag without reaching in. Handing it back to her, the man had given her a friendly and open smile. Anne had felt the flush that had been creeping up the back of her neck subside.

"Welcome to Mexico," he had said as she took the bag.

Then Anne was in Mexico, her first time in another country. It was easy to find her rental car, a little Volkswagen Bug that may have been born the same year as her. Her aunt had arranged everything, but Anne felt confident as she acted out the script Clara had written for her. It was her in Mexico, driving down a road by herself, following a map spread across the passenger seat. It was her parking and going inside to check into her room. It was definitely her walking by the pool and fantasizing about the dark young man lounging poolside. Clara may have been here before, but Anne was here now; besides, she couldn't imagine her aunt having an elaborate inner world full of fictional lovers. Anne was sure there was nothing normal about that.

She had almost turned and walked out when she saw the young man from the airplane checking in with his parents. Anne had hesitated at the door, fuming at her aunt for telling her that few tourists stayed here, fuming at herself for paying in advance for the whole week, and fuming at the young man for being handsome and forward and here. It had only taken a moment to mentally badger herself into relaxing and going with it, and the irony of the decision-making process had been lost on her as she pulled the door open.

Before she heard the door swing shut behind her, Anne had already felt the young man's eyes on her. He had spoken at the same time as the desk clerk, one in English and the other in Spanish.

"Are you following us?" The young man had been smirking.

"Un momento, por favor," the clerk had said, leaning to smile at her.

"Yo tengo una reservación," Anne had said, her face hot.

She had practiced that phrase all the way over here; apparently it was obvious to him.

"I'll be with you in a minute," the clerk had smiled, straightening. He had gone back to conversing with the couple, in English, and Anne made a big show of looking through a travel brochure near the front desk. The young man was looking at her the whole time; Anne had felt it. He had said something just as his parents turned with room keys in hand, and his words were lost in the sounds of their activity.

Ignoring him, Anne had stepped to the desk and smiled.

"I have a reservation," she had said. Anne could still feel him, watching her as he trailed his parents out the door. The clerk was looking at her expectantly. Anne had flushed again, realizing: she had already said that.

"Anne Miller," she had said. "Reservation for Anne Miller."

The moment she heard the door close behind him, Anne had relaxed. It was easy enough to get her key and room number, find her room, and haul in her bags. Finally in her room, with all of her things, Anne bolted the door and began to get undressed.

She had seen the young man with the dark skin and darker hair still lounging by the pool when she had brought her luggage in. The red and white bikini that Raina had talked her into buying was right on top of everything in her suitcase, and Anne had promised her friend that she would wear the skimpy ensemble at least once this trip. By the time the rest of her travel outfit had puddled to the floor, Anne had screwed up her courage to put it on and go talk to the boy at the pool.

Dressed only in her sandals, Anne kicked the dirty clothes into a ball and then kicked the ball into a corner. She unfolded the luggage rack and hefted her biggest travel bag onto it, unzipping it and throwing back the cover. There it was, smaller than she remembered, but with the same bright red and stark white. Anne picked up the two little pieces of fabric and stepped into the bathroom. The mirror was tall and wide, reflecting her nude body back at her nearly from the knees up.

Anne brushed her hair back over her shoulders and pushed her breasts forward. She tried to smile, but it looked as awkward as it felt. She tried to throw herself a smoldering look, but it looked silly too. Anne kept a straight face, her shoulders back and her breasts forward. She nodded. That's how she would approach him, with a serious face. Somehow Anne always thought she was prettiest when she looked a little unhappy, but she had decided long ago not to work on a pretty frown; she wanted to be happy.

"Hello," she said into the mirror, holding the forgotten bikini in one hand while the other brushed back her hair again. Anne cleared her throat, parted her legs a little, and let her eyes drift to her breasts. Her heart was pounding at the thought of talking to him, her nipples starting to harden visibly. Her hand moved to trace light circles around one of them.

"Hello," she said again. When she smiled this time, it was unbidden. It looked and felt more natural, and even a little sexy. Anne let her fingers brush her nipple lightly. It was harder, and her hand moved to tease the other one to a similar state as a realization struck her.

What if he doesn't speak English? Her hand hovered over her breast.

"Hola," Anne said, touching her nipple and feeling the hot shock of electrical sensations wash over her. She closed her eyes. Both of her hands were on her skin now, the bits of bikini hanging forgotten from her wrist as her hand moved to her other breast. Teasing herself, Anne let her own light touch tickle her belly before slipping between her legs.

She was so hot, one smoldering fire built on top of another built on top of another. Anne wondered if she should touch herself, as she did just that, or if she should save the building hunger for the boy by the pool. Maybe she might even give the American boy another chance, and brave his brazen nature rather than stammer nervously in another language. One thing was for sure: she wasn't going to meet anyone standing in front of the mirror touching herself. She could do that at home.

Still she touched herself, letting her feather touch trace lines along her belly and thighs in a slowly narrowing spiral. Her other hand was cupping her breast, kneading her own flesh with the first signs of urgency.

Anne opened her eyes as she opened her legs slightly further for her descending hand. She closed them again immediately, and let her mind create an image where she wasn't alone.

The sun was bright, both in the sky and in its reflection in the pool. Anne saw herself, framed in light, strolling along the water's edge. She could see the dark young man look up as she approached, but she kept her eyes on the glinting water. The red and white bikini looked perfect on her, and Anne felt confident putting one sandaled foot in front of the other. Her legs moved slowly, energized by the feel of his eyes on them. Her shoulders back, Anne's breasts were pushed forward just enough to invite his gaze to travel upward.

As she neared, Anne could feel his eyes explore the contours of her body. From her shifting legs to her flat belly and then to her rounded breasts, he took her in. When she stopped in front of him, his eyes slowly travelled from her breasts to her eyes.

He smiled. "Hello, beautiful girl."

Anne had her serious face on, even in her fantasy, and she slowly brought one finger to her lips. Slowly, wordlessly, she shushed him. Placing her hands on her hips to accentuate her smooth curves, Anne looked back meaningfully over her shoulder. She could see the rear door to her room from here, the sliding glass that opened onto the pool. When her eyes found his again, he received her silent message.

The young man raised himself on the lounge chair, then stood. Anne watched his muscles twitch and flex as he shifted, then watched him raise himself to his full height. Now he was looking down at her a little, still smiling. He had nothing but swim trunks on, and Anne let her eyes travel shamelessly over his slim chest and arms. Still she kept a straight face.

Slowly, Anne reached out to take his hand. The moment their skin touched, she turned and led him toward the sliding glass. In the few steps they had to take before they reached the doorway, Anne watched her fantasy from two perspectives. One part of her felt his hand in hers, saw the door to her room getting closer and closer, and was acutely aware of both. The other part of her watched from afar, noting how handsome he was and how slim she looked as they walked together.

Her free hand touched the door handle, and Anne's observing view watched him follow her into the room. From outside, she saw the young man from the airplane watching them enter the room together. He looked sad and hurt, and Anne took a moment to console herself with the fact that none of this was real before putting her whole attention on the scene in her room. He was opening his mouth to speak again, and Anne was putting her finger over his lips this time. They were soft, and smiling.

Anne stepped into him, raising herself on her tiptoes to meet his mouth with hers. She felt his flesh pressing into hers, his naked chest against her slim top. In her mind, it was easy to move while she kissed him, her mouth on his while she undid her top and then moving down his slim tan torso as she slid off her bottoms and then his. Moving easily to her knees, Anne looked up at him with her face alongside his hardness. She smiled, then turned her head and kissed it lightly.

Her hand was between her legs as she kissed him up one side and down the other. The kisses were soft and light, but every one of them seemed to make him harder and harder. Anne's fingers were kneading the engorged flesh around her mounting hunger, and they were slick with her desire. Her touches pressed into the wet folds of heat as she took him in her mouth.

Anne moaned.

There was a loud rapping at the front door, followed by a friendly shouted voice.

"Room service!"

Anne's arms went into a defensive cross over her breasts as her mind snapped back into the actual moment.

"Just a minute!" she called out. "I'm in the shower!"

She caught a glimpse of herself in the mirror, arms crossed to hide all of her nakedness except that growing vortex of hunger. Anne looked at herself for a second, noting for the hundred-thousandth time how different she looked when she was turned on. That ever-blossoming flower seemed to be the cause of both her deepest torment and her greatest pleasure. Without having felt it, Anne wondered if she could survive the next level of her desire. Would a man's touch make her explode when it finally found her? Would feeling him inside her cause Anne to burst apart into a million happily scintillating pieces? Or would it put out the fire at last, and ignite in her some other passion that did not follow every wave of pleasure with a tsunami of guilt?

Wrapping a towel about her, Anne checked her hair in the mirror before crossing the room to open the door.

Who knows? Anne thought in the most private recesses of her mind. *Maybe it's the boy from the pool. Maybe he works here. Maybe I'm about to find out what it's like after all.*

It wasn't the boy from the pool; it was the middle-aged chubby guy from the front desk. He was smiling and bearing aloft a stack of two large white towels topped by a spare roll of toilet paper.

"Towels for by the pool," he explained, still smiling. One of his teeth glinted gold in the sunlight. He looked pointedly at her hair.

"I thought you said you were in the shower," he mused.

Anne took the stack of sundries.

"Thanks," she blurted, slamming the door in his face.

CHAPTER 7

The sun was not as high in the sky when Anne finally made it out to the pool. The handsome dark young man was gone too. Just as well; Anne felt like she was trying to hide the generous amount of skin the red and white bikini was showing off by shrinking into herself as much as possible. She knew she wasn't the slim and sexy version of herself that had come out here earlier in her mind. Instead, Anne was the self-conscious young bundle of insecurities that she was accustomed to filling out her form. She couldn't take a full breath, much less throw her shoulders back with confidence. Arms crossed over the vast expanse of naked skin between the two scant pieces of fabric, she walked along the deserted poolside.

Anne found a lounger that was still in the dwindling sunlight and spread her towel over it. The sun would slide past her spot in the next hour or so; no need to put on sunblock or glasses. Propping the back of the lounger to a sitting position, Anne opened her diary on her lap. She found the next blank page and wrote the date at the top. The numbers were squiggly under her uncertain hand.

Sighing, Anne got up and adjusted the lounge chair once more. Laying it flat, she turned to lie facedown on the towel. Her eyes and nose hung over the end, and her arms snaked around either side. One hand held the book open, the other held her pen. It wasn't the ideal position, but at least it was stable. As per usual, Anne began the entry with a description of her surroundings. Too many entries began with "I am sitting in bed, alone in my own bedroom, alone in my own home." She was excited for a new beginning. Anne wrote:

I am lounging by a pool in Mexico! The flight was pretty horrific, and the motel came with its own set of complications, but I'm here! All by myself in Mexico! I have to lay in a kind of awkward position to write this, and most of my ass is hanging out of my tiny little bikini, but there is no one around anyway. There was a cute Mexican boy out here earlier, but he's gone. Sigh...

In case you hadn't guessed, I'm still a virgin. I imagined losing it to two total strangers today, which I suppose is better than imagining losing it to Henry over and over. To tell the truth, I haven't thought much of Henry at all today, except to compare him to the boy on the plane. Now that was a fantasy to end all fantasies! It was so embarrassing; I fell asleep on the plane and had the most intense dream. A handsome young stranger, the one I was comparing to Henry before I fell asleep, followed me into the bathroom. It seemed so real, I could feel his touch and his kisses like never before! It seemed so real that I kept thinking about how I was losing my virginity, and how different it felt than when I had imagined it all those times.

I was moaning and whimpering like crazy in the dream, and I think I might have been doing it in my sleep on the plane too. I felt the most incredible orgasm building inside of me; I can't imagine the noise I would have made if I hadn't woke up when I did.

Oh, and get this: he's staying at the same motel as me! With his parents! Ugh! Oh well, I hadn't planned on spending much time here anyway. I didn't come to Mexico to sit by a pool and fall for some boring boy from California like me. Tomorrow it's adventure time! I'll chart a course and follow it all day, go somewhere where I have to test my crappy Spanish...maybe meet a nice Mexican boy? Maybe meet a not-so-nice Mexican boy? I don't want a cartel gangster or anything, but I don't need a Mexican version of Henry either.

Alright, new vacation rule: No more thinking of Henry, or Raina, or Henry and Raina; and no more mention of it in my journal even if I do think of it. I am on vacation from perfect Henry and his perfect old-fashioned name and his perfect old-fashioned family and his perfect old-fashioned girlfriend. This is officially me time.

Speaking of "me time", I have not started touching myself once in the last three days without being interrupted. I feel like I'm going to boil over like a volcano. I keep building up steam, then someone calls or knocks on the door, or I wake up. How ridiculous is it to say you feel super horny when you've never even had a guy touch you? I want it so bad...you know, that thing I've never had. Sounds silly, right?

You should have seen the boy by the pool. He looked even more handsome than the boy on the plane, though not as tall. I don't know, it was hard to tell; he was laying on a lounger by the pool. I went into my room after I saw him and started touching myself. I was so close to feeling that tension inside *of me release all over my own fingers, in a typical fantasy in my typical fashion. Then there was a*

"Hey," a voice behind her said, startling Anne. She slammed the notebook shut and twisted awkwardly on the lounger. It was the young man from the plane, tall and framed in sunlight.

Anne turned all the way over and tried to lay back to make her belly look as flat as possible. She looked up at him, squinting in the sunlight.

"Hey," Anne said quietly. She clutched the book to her breasts.

"I don't think we started off on the right foot," he said. He smiled, and looked even more handsome and compelling for it.

"Um," Anne responded, using up all of the vocabulary she currently had.

"Do you want to grab something to eat together?" His smile was inviting, his eyebrows raised hopefully.

Anne's mind raced, but somehow none of her thoughts could be translated into speech. She tried for a moment to order them, to corral the wild herd of ideas so she might select one to ride. After a moment she gave up, opened her mouth and let whatever words that might spill out do so.

"Sorry, I have plans," she blurted. "I need to go get ready."

Standing abruptly, Anne noted again how tall he was, how handsome. She brushed past him, feeling her whole body flush as she gathered up her towel and headed for the sliding glass entrance to her room. His eyes were on her as she walked away, she could feel it. Her legs didn't want to work right, and Anne had to think simple mechanical thoughts to coax simple mechanical motion from them. She knew that most of her butt was hanging out there for him to see, but she tried not to think of it as she crossed the seemingly endless space between herself and her room. She was nearly to the door when he called out, making her start visibly.

"Maybe later," he said behind her. "Hey, my name is Todd."

Anne didn't turn or call her name back to him. She slid the door open, stepped through and closed it behind her. Heart pounding, she swept the curtains closed over the tall glass. She breathed, coming back to herself at last. She was hungry, Anne realized it now. But what could she do? Go back out and tell him that his handsome tallness had made her so nervous that she had blown him off? Explain that under the bundle of insecurities that floated on her surface was a deep dark ocean of desire? Ask him to skip dinner and feed her growing nether hunger instead? Anything she thought of was too bold or too silly to consider, and after a few minutes she stopped trying. She also gave up on getting dinner; Anne had no doubt that whatever restaurant she chose would somehow be the same one he chose. She flushed again at the thought of sitting at a table alone across from him with his parents or some beautiful young Mexican girl.

She was still in her bikini. For some reason she wrapped the wide towel around her, like she should have done out there. It wasn't cold in here, and she didn't need any more privacy than she had; Anne just didn't want to look at her mostly nude body right now. Not thinking, she flipped on the television. It was in Spanish, of course, and she flipped it off a moment later. Anne doffed her sandals and sat cross-legged on the bed, the towel wrapped about her like a blanket.

Ignoring her grumbling belly, Anne opened the journal in front of her on the bed. Rather than finish the entry she had started, she flipped through old pages and read some of her previous entries.

The journal had been one of her punishments for her parents' passing. There had been rewards, if you could call them that: the life insurance policies had paid off the house and gave Anne all the money she needed to finish high school and attend college after. She had been able to live her life just as it had been before, only without her parents, as long as she jumped through the hoops that were her punishment.

Going to a counselor twice a week had been the most grueling part; Anne was raised by parents who thought that whatever they needed to work out should be worked out in the safety and privacy of their own minds. She had taken to the practice like a fish to water, and talking about her feelings for an hour twice a week with a perfect stranger had seemed an affront to their memory. Anne learned to get comfortable being uncomfortable in the woman's office, under her watchful gaze and penetrating questions. When the counselor had told her that they could go to once a week if Anne wrote in a journal every day, she had jumped at any opportunity to lessen the torment. She was further relieved when the woman explained that she would never ask to read the entries, only to see that she had written something every day.

There was only one thing that Anne could say was a constant in her life, and that was her fantasies. She had had grief over her parents, grief that made her feel like she was viewing the world through a small porthole that lie just beyond her reach. Talking about it and writing about it didn't make it go away, but sitting with it every night in her empty house changed her relationship with her grief over time. Sometimes she would cry, other times she would just close her eyes and let the memories and thoughts and feelings scroll across her inner theater. That seemed to help, or maybe it had been the grueling talks; either way, at some point Anne began to see the world as being all around her once more. Her grief over her parents became a somber melancholy within her, the tender hurt covered over finally with emotional scar tissue.

All that time she had spent healing, Anne had also written every day in her journal. She had filled the pages with her fantasies, mostly all the ways she had imagined losing her virginity to Henry. Some were sweet wonderings, especially in the beginning; they were filled with hugs and kisses and all the the pretty words she wished someone would say to her. As time went on, Anne's curiosity and hunger had found voice in those private pages. She thought as she paged through some of the entries that they might make even the most sexually experienced woman flush.

Unfortunately, they were having no effect on her. The warm thrill that tickled her insides when she read or wrote about her unreal exploits was absent today; they were just words on pages, as flat and two-dimensional as her actual sex life. The hunger inside of her was not crying out for her fantasies, or her fingers, and her attempts to engage it with tasteless appetizers was only adding fuel to the inferno.

Anne sighed, put aside the book and climbed under the covers. Lying there, still wrapped in bikini and towel under the blankets, she closed her eyes and immersed herself in her own turmoil. The hunger in her belly grumbled at her, the hunger in her center gnawed at her, and it was a good long time before Anne fell asleep.

CHAPTER 8

nne was awake before the sun came up. Rather than dawdle in bed or finger herself into further frustration, she headed straight for the shower. It was all business there too, although she did throw a wistful glance at the detachable shower head at one point. She giggled while she washed her hair, thinking that her own shower head at home might get jealous if she put another between her legs. Then she considered the possibility that some other guest had used it for the same purpose, and frowned all through conditioning her hair.

The map showed mountains and valleys as well as cities and their populations. Anne drew a fairly straight line down a long highway with her blue highlighter. She considered an overnight bag in the car, just in case; but she thought it might be more romantic if she didn't have it. If something happened. She might just drive all day, only get out to get gas, and see how far she could get before feeling like she ought to turn around.

A beautiful sunrise greeted her as Anne pulled onto the highway, and she took it as a good omen. She felt the tension of a restless night start to leave her as the miles ticked past, and she left the radio off to listen to her own happy and hopeful thoughts. Nearly a hundred miles from her hotel, she finally stopped to eat her first meal since leaving Maysville. She knew how to say chicken in Spanish, so that's what she ate for breakfast. The rest of the food that covered her plate was not her usual morning fare, but it was delicious and she was hungry.

Anne had to force herself to eat slowly. The little outdoor hut that she was eating in was full of men with dark skin and dark eyes that were all turned her way. There were a couple of women there, and a few kids, but they were no different. The women didn't smack or scold their men or their children; they stared right along with them. For the first time Anne had a small inkling of what a newcomer felt like in Maysville. To tell the truth, she kind of liked it. They were friendly eyes, and the wondering thoughts behind them felt friendly too. Every time she met eyes with someone, she smiled; and every time, they smiled back. It was kind of magical.

There weren't a lot of young guys, but there was one handsome fellow that looked like he was surely less than thirty. When Anne met eyes with him, he smiled first. When she smiled back, he grinned broadly and sat up straighter in his seat. She glowed at the response while she picked over the last of her breakfast. From the corner of her eye she filed away little bits of information about him for later: the way his hair fell in his face, how his eyes had sparkled when he smiled, the shape and size of his hands. By the time she smiled shyly at him on the way out, Anne knew what she would be doing tonight if fate didn't bring a more substantial encounter her way.

With her mind spinning a story about the stranger, it was a good long while before Anne noticed that she was not on the same road as before. She quailed inside for a moment, then felt her confidence spring forth anew. The sun had been to her left before; now it was behind her. She had headed east without realizing it. Anne considered going back, briefly, but decided to go with it instead. She would stop at the next town and re-orient.

There was another long stretch of driving before Anne noticed that she hadn't seen another car or a sign for miles, followed by an even longer stretch before the road began to show signs of serious disrepair. She drove slowly for another mile, looking for a place to turn around while avoiding potholes and vegetation that had grown up through the cracked pavement. There was another little road, more overgrown than this one, intersecting it up ahead. Anne pulled past it a little and backed carefully up the other path. She had a horrifying image of herself getting stuck out here in the middle of nowhere, but the road held firm.

Anne backed up even further and parked the car. She shut off the engine, but left the keys in the ignition; she wasn't going far. She grabbed a couple of tissues from her purse and stood for the first time in a good while. Taking a few cautious steps into the unfamiliar vegetation, Anne scanned the terrain for a clear open spot to empty her bladder. There was no way she was making it back to town.

It was only a few more steps to do it near the base of a nearby hillside. Anne moved towards it, and couldn't take her eyes off the sharply rising rock face as she unfastened and squatted. Something about it seemed unnatural somehow; and even as she wiped herself, Anne scanned every square inch that she could see from where she squatted. When she pulled up her underwear and jeans, Anne got a whole new perspective.

She gasped. The moss *was* moving. Taking a step forward, she wiped away some viney vegetation and resisted the urge to gasp once more. There was an opening there, a dark opening into a cave that looked like it went pretty far back. Excited, she hurried back to the car to get the keys and the little flashlight she carried in her purse. Anne grinned as she rolled up the windows and locked the little bug.

"This is what I'm here for," she muttered happily. "An adventure."

Anne hardly hesitated at the mouth of the cave, and soon she was enveloped in cool dank underground air. It felt nice after the heat, cool comfort in the endless darkness. The tunnel was tall and wide, and Anne walked for quite a ways along the soft sand underfoot before coming to a fork. This far down the path, there were no sounds but her falling footsteps. The building storm outside rumbled closer and louder with each passing moment, but none of the noise found its way this far underground. Even as the sky lit up with bright flashes and fat raindrops began to fall, Anne heard none of it. She ventured to the left and further down the path, bringing her deeper into the earth.

CHAPTER 9

There seemed to be no end to the slowly descending path. Anne walked past another two forks that went off into the darkness down slightly smaller tunnels. It was clear that this was no ordinary cave, and it became clearer the longer she walked. First were the torches hanging from the walls at regular intervals; they looked like they had hung unlit for an awfully long time, but they had brightened these hallways for someone at some point. Then there were the symbols etched into the walls; they were carefully carved, either painstakingly by hand or with some power tool that predated electricity. She could tell this place was not entirely natural, and that the last time it had bustled with any serious activity had been long before she was born. Besides that, the subterranean space was layers of mystery to her.

Anne checked her watch, trying to remember how long she had been walking. For the first time the thought of fear came to mind; but it was just a thought, banished quickly by her excitement. She pressed on until her flashlight began to flicker and her steps became slower and more hesitant. Just as she was about to turn back, the tunnel opened into a vast wide space. It took her breath away, and turned her flashlight into a dim searchlight that stabbed uselessly at endless inky blackness.

Tracing her way along the tall wall, Anne could see more torches hanging along the gradual curvature that she was following. The ceiling was too high up for her failing flashlight to illuminate, and the middle of the huge circular space similarly danced just beyond the dimming light as well. Anne walked the whole perimeter without seeing much of anything except two smaller passageways that dove even deeper into the earth. She decided while she circled that she would head back as soon as she reached the passage she had taken here; as much as the continuing paths intrigued her, it was time to get back. Even more, Anne felt drawn to the mysterious center of the room. She was certain there was something more than just sand and wide open space in here, but she couldn't say why.

Anne was back where she had started. She took two steps away from the exit, shining the flashlight towards the center of the space. For a moment she thought she saw a flash of white, some shape taking form behind it it the dark; then the flashlight flickered, the shadows shifted, and all she could see was sand and dark. Anne sighed and turned her back on the mystery. There was no way she was going to the center of a circular room with three nearly identical passageways to see if there was something interesting enough there to disorient her. The only trail she could leave were clothes, being fresh out of breadcrumbs. She had left her jacket at the one junction that might have confused her coming out, and Anne didn't feel like doffing her top or her jeans to mark another.

Making her way back to the surface, Anne debated what she would do next. Her mind racing noisily in the silence, one part of her argued that some mysteries are best left mysteries. This place was the business of an archaeological crew, not a young woman on vacation. Besides, it wasn't that far off the road or that hard to find; surely whatever was once in the huge space and the passages beyond had been removed long ago by professionals or thieves. She might be trespassing, or risk causing the cave walls to tumble in on her with her activities. There were endless reasons to leave this place and never come back, and that one part of her listed them as she walked.

There was another part of her there too. It was a small part, but it was still there. It reminded her that things would never change if she didn't. It asked her if she would rather live a long life of boring safety or a short life of excitement. It pointed out how ironic it would be if some great mystery that was waiting to change her life awaited in the dark of that space, or the passages beyond, and she had walked away after being so close. There had been *something* there, that was no trick of the light; it was not caution or reason that had turned her around…it was fear. It was the same fear that kept her in the little town she had grown up in, the same fear that kept her from telling Henry or Raina or anybody how she really felt, the same fear that kept every man that might want to touch her at arm's length.

The voices battled in her head, the one that controlled her life and the one that cried out for change deafening her in the stillness. The second voice had been growing stronger lately; it was the reason she was in Mexico in the first place. But the first was so loud, and so accustomed to being in charge, that Anne had resigned herself to leaving this place forever long before she reached the mouth of the cave. If it weren't for the darkened sky and pounding sheets of rain outside, she would have surely gotten in the rental car and driven away.

When she stepped from the darkness Anne was immediately drenched. The rain was as warm as it was wet, and the drumming beat of drops on her head seemed to wash away the whirling thoughts in her head. For a full minute she stood out in it, her arms out and her head tilted back to face the downpour. It soaked her hair through to her scalp, soaked through her top and jeans and then through her bra and panties, until streams of water coursed between her clothes and her skin like a warm rushing river. Anne felt cleansed, renewed, and peaceful in an odd energized way. Her mind was as quiet as the cave.

She could see the car, but just barely. It was hard to tell if night was falling or if the storm was all that darkened the sky; either way the effect was the same. Anne took a few steps past the car to shine the last few rays of the flashlight up the main road, but all she could see was falling rain. Every direction looked the same, layered darkness or a sheet of reflected light. With no sun in the sky she couldn't be certain which way she had come or which way she needed to go, even if she could see the road.

Anne took a deep breath and sighed it out there in the drumming downpour. She wasn't afraid or uncertain; she knew she would just have to wait it out. The only question that remained was whether she would wait it out in the car or wait it out in the intriguing network of subterranean passages that called to her from the hillside.

CHAPTER 10

A few steps into the cave, Anne stopped to undress. She was soaked through with warm cleansing rain, and so were her clothes. She set her purse on the ground, dug a little hole in the sand and placed the flashlight in it. There was little more than a ghostly glow emanating from it. The light would brighten momentarily if she smacked the back of her hand against it, only to fade once more to a ghostly glow. Anne undressed in the wan light as quickly as she could, wringing out her clothes and hanging them from the first small outcropping of stone that held a torch.

Grasping the torch and removing it carefully, Anne lowered herself to her knees in the sand next to her bag. Opening it, she pushed aside the soiled airplane panties that she had forgotten to ball up with the rest of her laundry. There was a little pocket knife, which she didn't need right now, and two full books of matches. Anne took one out and set the purse aside, then set about trying to get one of the little paper fire-starters to light and stay lit. She got it on the third try, but it went out as soon as she touched the flame to the torch.

Weaving the ineffective rejects into the torch's reeds along with two unlit matches, Anne was able to get each little stub going with the next match she struck. To her amazement, she was soon staring at a controlled blaze that lit the cave far better that her flashlight ever could. She raised herself to her full height, torch in hand, and watched her own nude form in dancing shadow against the cave wall. Anne felt primal and alive, unafraid and unashamed. She lit another torch from the first and hung it by her clothes. It was cooler in the cave than it was out in the warm wet rain, but it was a comfortable coolness that tickled rather than prickled her naked skin.

Without hesitation, she went along the path she had followed earlier, lighting every third or fourth torch as she did. There was no need to drop breadcrumbs now, or scraps of clothes she didn't have. Anne strode confidently down the lighted tunnel from one torch to the next, watching her own slim shapeliness in the shadows every time she stretched to spark another fire. Her skin was prickly now, but it was prickly with reawakened desire. Anne's nipples stood out stiff and firm as she moved swiftly down the path, and the only reason she looked back was to see the sensual shifting movements of her buttocks and legs as they flexed and moved.

Every step she took seemed to make her skin more sensitive to the still damp air, to the warmth of her torch, to the sand under her feet. Every cell of her body was tingling with exquisitely pleasured awareness, and every torch she lit was feeding the fire within her. Anne wondered for a moment if she was in one of her own fantasies, dreaming only to wake in Maysville a normal boring girl with a wild imagination. Then she reminded herself that she was alone. She was never alone in her fantasies; that's why she had them.

Anne came upon the circular space sooner this time, moving more quickly towards it in her naked confidence. By the time she stepped through the doorway every part of her was blazing as hot as the torch. She wasn't sure just what she was doing as she walked the perimeter, lighting every torch that she encountered as she moved without thought. When Anne had lit them all, the room began to warm up almost immediately. The ring of fire cast a sensual glow over her and most of the space, but the high ceiling and the far center were still swathed in darkness.

Holding her own torch aloft, Anne felt her spine straighten and her shoulders go back as she put one foot forward. She looked out first, toward the dark middle, then shifted slightly to take another step. Her own flexing muscles caught her eye, and in her heightened state of awareness Anne didn't feel self-conscious about admiring her own beauty. The heat from the torches was meeting the burn of her hunger at the surface of her skin, and a thin sheen of sweat had formed between her breasts. As she watched, a bead of perspiration formed and raced rapidly over her belly to disappear into her thin landing strip.

Leaning back, looking down at her own naked body, Anne swung the torch slowly back and forth in front of her. She turned and flexed her calves and thighs, then stood with her legs spread a little and her hips pushed forward. Anne had always thought her hips were too big, her breasts too small; the stranger looking out from behind her eyes thought nothing of the sort. Her eyes looked over her own body hungrily, and the hand not holding the torch drifted over her belly and breasts like an artist lovingly shaping clay.

Still watching herself, still touching herself, Anne began to walk toward the center of the room. She was almost upon the body before she even noticed it. Rather than scream, or run, or have even a flicker of fear, Anne knelt in the sand next to the hooded corpse. She felt the way her breasts shifted when she leaned forward, the way her wet folds moved and spread when she squatted. Her fingers were sensitive like every other part of her right now, but pushing back the hood was a tingling excitement rather than a disgusting chore. Even the skull underneath was not a surprise, nor did it frighten her; Anne stared calmly at it, as if she had expected to find it.

"Not a hood," Anne murmured. "Not a hood, but a habit."

Her own voice almost brought Anne back to herself, to a place where she could see herself kneeling nude in front of a corpse with a blazing torch in her hand and be appropriately shocked. It was low and throaty, raw and hoarse from the heat or her hunger or both. Instead the next sound that came from her was a happy quiet growl, or a loud purr, and she held the torch even higher while she leaned in even closer.

The cloak she had thought she had seen was a nun's habit, thick folds of dark cloth covered in a thin skiff of dust that drifted under Anne's hot breath. The hood she had removed was her headpiece, and it had slid off the skinless head to drop to the floor behind the corpse. She was arranged comfortably, presuming she was a she, on a flat stone pedestal that supported her kneeling pose even in death. A low back and several stiff and dusty cushions held her from falling back or to the side, and she was leaned back into them with her arms over her chest. The skeletal remains of her fingers clasped her own shoulders, most of them covered by the long thick sleeves.

Anne grasped one of her wrists through the thick coarse fabric, and moved it gently to rest in the corpse's lap. She saw it more clearly now, a tome bound in thick rough dark leather. Anne had to pull harder at the other hand; it refused to come loose from the dead shoulder, almost like the corpse was trying to hold onto the book. Or stop Anne from reading it.

Something had taken shape in Anne during the long naked walk here, something primal and urgent and overwhelming. Nothing was going to stop her from getting that book, or anything else she would ever want. The fire within her was ready to blaze a path from her to her desires, setting aflame anything that dared stand in her way. Just as Anne readied her new certainty to level it at the corpse, prepared to splinter bones or break them to powder, the hand came easily from the shoulder it had been clutching. It was as if she had felt Anne's determination, and given up the fight.

Then Anne was on her knees before the corpse, ignoring the deep hollows of its eyes as they watched her examine the book. The cover was hard to the touch, ancient leather that had turned to unyielding stone with the passing years. There were words on it, or symbols in groupings that looked like words, but Anne could neither read them nor identify the language. She frowned, disappointed, and turned to the first page. It was thick, and stiff, and unlike any kind of paper she had ever seen; the pages seemed like thin glass, impossibly brittle, but they held up to her gentle handling. The writing on them was more symbols that looked like nonsense to her; but she marveled at the beauty and the delicacy of the pages as she slowly turned them, examining the strange relic carefully.

On the third page the writing changed somewhat. Rather than tight groupings of symbols that resembled paragraphs, it looked like a recipe or set of instructions. It was the same handwriting, in the same dull crispy brown ink, but the sentences were short and widely spaced. Anne still couldn't read a word of it, or even a letter. She turned the page.

Now *those* were letters. Anne leaned forward further, bringing the torch in closer. It wasn't English, but it was definitely Italian or Spanish or French or some other Latin-based language. Most of the letters were familiar to her, but the groupings were completely foreign. It was clearly written in a different hand than the first three pages, a flowing cursive that looked like textbook handwriting. Had she stopped to think, she would have wished Raina were here. She had gotten Anne through two years of Spanish, and Anne had gotten her through algebra. She didn't stop, though, or think of Raina. Anne would have guessed it was a woman's writing if she had to, but she didn't have to. She turned the page.

The letters were the same on the next page, foreign words in plain print, yet another hand at work in the book. There were six pages like that altogether, all in what looked like the same language but each in a uniquely different style of handwriting. As she leafed through them, Anne noticed that the ink was changing color on the brittle pages as she turned them. The first few entries had been that same dried brown, with a flaky rigid texture that she could feel rising over the flat cold pages. As the entries progressed, the ink was getting lighter in color and more liquid in texture. At some point what she had suspected from the beginning became clear: the book had been written in blood.

Still she didn't feel a flicker of fear. Anne turned the page again, and again leaned in closer. The words looked familiar, more familiar but more foreign at the same time. The letters were both right and wrong, and words tried to leap out at her from the jumbled characters. Anne narrowed her eyes, willing the answer to come. Then it did, and she let out another happy low growl. It was English, but it was backwards. Anne was looking at the mirror image of a document somehow, written in yet another unfamiliar hand but written in her language at least.

She lay the book flat on the sand at the corpse's feet,

open to the backward page. Anne worked the narrow unlit end of the torch into the sand and crouched on her elbows and knees, her head over the book with her hands in the sand on either side of it. The cavern had grown even warmer, and a slippery layer of sweat covered her entire nude crouching form. Her hard nipples brushed against the sand, her ribcage going wide with every one of her deep unconscious breaths, to gather little grains of white. Her knees were parted slightly in the sand, so the most hot and wet part of her could feel the waves of heat flooding the room. The curve of her rounded bottom rose over the curve of her shoulder, with the deep arched curve of her back between them.

Anne looked like an animal ready to pounce, either on food or flesh bent to some other purpose. Instead she hovered, perfectly still, in the most sensual pose no one could see. Even she was not aware of it, such was her concentration. A small pool of perspiration formed in the arched small of her glistening back, but she didn't notice that either. All of her attention was focused on reading the backward message, despite the fact that her body virtually crackled with the intensity of her lifetime of desire.

A few words came clear, then a few more; but by then the first few had skittered from her mind. Anne went back to the beginning, at the top right of the page, and read aloud in a hoarse husky whisper.

"When I died," she read, "everyone who knew me knew me as Sister Theresa. Before that, my name was Clare Anne. Due to my shame, and to protect my family's good standing, I will not give my surname here."

Anne paused. They were both common enough names, of course, and probably often paired together. But they were both familiar names as well, two of the small handful of monikers that her own family tree chose from when labeling their daughters for life. Her mother's mother used to tell her stories about the women that had come before her along maternal branches. She always called them the "Manchester Women", though she admitted freely that none of the women in her stories carried that particular surname. They all had the same five first two names, Abigail or Esther, Mary or Clare…or, of course, Anne. The rebel daughters sometimes went so far as to name their babies versions of the names, Anna or Maria or Clara; but according to her grandmother, those deviations were always punished in the end. She wouldn't say how, but she sure behaved as though the stories she refused to tell were important and somehow dangerously exciting.

Anne was suddenly overcome with exhaustion. Her taut crouch relaxed, and she lowered her hips while raising her shoulders. Looking around in a slow circle, her eyelids drooping halfway over her eyes, Anne watched the flickering flames that dotted the far wall. She felt the heat all around her, she felt it climbing inside of her, and she crouched seductively once more to feel it lap at her naked and glistening folds of flesh. One of her arms was bent, buried partially in the sand from elbow to wrist as she leaned into it. The other hand brushed back the wet stringing strands of her own dark hair that clung in clumps to her face and shoulders.

The sand that had covered her hand was dislodged by her hair and the slippery path it took down her torso. Over her breasts and pounding heartbeat her fingers glided, touching here and grasping there, until her hand slid between her thighs to bury itself in slick stickiness. It was harder than ever not to slip her finger inside, although her whole body was already tensing in anticipation of an intense climax from her first flickering touches.

As her hand moved between her legs in a slow steady

rhythm, Anne let a low moan escape her lips. It went on for several seconds, rising in pitch and volume as her fingers moved with more pressure and speed. Her eyes were open, her whole attention on her pounding heart and electric skin and the pleasure of her own desperate touch. The low rolling sound echoed back at her from the far walls as her body began to tremble, and she continued to vibrate pleasurably as she collapsed sideways on the sand. Her entire frame went from tense and crouching to relaxed and splayed on the sand, with sublime tingles dancing ecstasy over her skin.

She had no thought for comfort, except to enjoy the afterglow and cast about with sleepy eyes for something to lay her head on. The only thing nearby was the book, and she noticed as she reached for it that three of her fingers were streaked in blood. Her purse was hanging alongside her clothes, and Anne didn't have it in her to go back for either. She grasped the book with bloody fingers and dragged it across the sand.

Resting the soft flushed skin of her cheek on the rough leather cover felt somewhat abrasive, so Anne opened to the first page. Its glassy fragility felt good, cold and smooth on her hot flesh. Anne turned to the second page, so the cool touch of the other page would be there if she turned her head in her sleep. She was getting blood on the book, but she didn't have the energy or the material to wipe it clean. Anne rested her head on the splayed pages and drifted immediately into a pleasantly deep sleep.

CHAPTER 11

Anne woke before she woke, becoming aware of her surroundings without being able to move her limbs or open her eyes. She remembered where she was, and what had happened last night, but she couldn't look to inspect the mess or move to clean it.

While she lay there frozen, she heard the crackling fire of the torches, still burning somehow. She felt the smooth surface of the book's open pages, cool under her cheek. Anne willed herself to move, first all of her and then individual parts of her, but she continued to lay still. Although her prone form was motionless silence, her internal efforts were struggled cacophony. It took her a few moments before she realized that there was a sound in the mix that was coming from outside herself.

Quieting her inner turmoil, Anne listened intently. She forced her mind to be as still as her body and focused her attention on listening.

There it was again, the scuffling sound of footfalls or something being dragged slowly across the sand. She tried to hear a pattern in the footsteps, listened to see if it was two feet or four, tried to judge the size of whatever was moving closer. Nothing made sense in her feared paralysis; the only thing clear was that it was indeed approaching her as she lay waiting. The steps became more confident as they neared, and when they stopped Anne could hear steady labored breathing.

Whatever it was stood over her. The only sound it made was a whistling wind as it breathed in, followed by the sighed grunt of an exhale. Anne listened to the pattern, wondering what kind of strange animal or stranger person would breathe like that or stand motionless over her naked body so long. Then it moved, and she prepared herself to be clawed or bitten as best she could without being able to move at all. She felt a face over her hand; the hand covered in blood, and Anne's thick secret flavor layered one over the other. Hot breath tickled her fingers, but no tongue licked at them and no teeth bit at them. Instead the hot breath and eerie closeness slipped past her wrist, slowly moving up her arm to linger once again when it reached her shoulder.

Now it did touch her, nuzzling or brushing back a lock of her hair. The touch was surprisingly gentle, whatever it was. Anne had as little control over her feelings as she did her body; and as the breath moved again, she watched both from the inside with detached curiosity.

Her body was responding to the breath, her skin starting to flush everywhere it fell on her. Tickling pleasantness spread from each place that the breath landed, a network of electricity that was causing her blood to flow faster as her own breath came hotter. She didn't just lack physical control; she had somehow surrendered it to this place, or this creature. All of her fear left her as she came to a wordless understanding in her mind. Something told her that everything would be okay if she just relaxed, so somehow that's what she did.

The breath moved over her hair and down her back, tracing the line of her spine as Anne lay unmoving on her side. She felt those excited thrills that each breath set off shooting out in every direction to collide and explode in pleasurable bursts all over her body. Though the hand or nose that had touched her before brushed her skin lightly a few more times, she could not tell what or who was doing the touching. Anne only knew that it was tender, and slow, and comforting in some way she had never known.

One of her legs was straight along the sand, the other bent so her knee rested on the sand while one ankle crossed over the other. The breath moved from the small of her back to her hips, and that gentle touch brushed her bent knee as it traveled down Anne's leg. The breath paused at her feet, and Anne felt mild tickles combine with the excited thrills to travel rapidly from the bottoms of her feet like fireworks to explode pleasured shocks in her brain. She felt the breath follow the electricity, slowly riding the ecstatic current up the inside of her other leg.

It paused at the back of her knee, and Anne felt another soft comforting moment of contact. Then it moved along her inner thigh, until Anne had the thought that if it moved any closer it would taste her where her flavor was the strongest. She thought of the blood, and her immobility, but only for a moment. Soon she was overwhelmed by the warm flowing feel of sensual tingles over her entire body. It felt like she was taking a shower, only the warm clean flow traveled over her and through her and upward towards her head. The silent symphony climaxed in her mind, clearing her head until nothing remained but a pleasing spacious hum.

The breath was gone; her body was her own again.

Anne sat up, suddenly, searching the shadows with her eyes. The room was empty, the sand around her as bare as her naked skin. She inspected the ground around her carefully, looking for footprints or paw tracks. The only marks were the ones she had made: a straight line of little footprints that led here, and her deep elbow and knee marks in the sand. No man had been here, and no animal either. She must have been dreaming.

Rising easily, Anne marveled at the electrical hum that had stayed with her. She watched her mind, quietly alert, while her body moved with fluid confidence. She hardly noticed the dried sweat and blood on her, somehow feeling clean and refreshed like never before despite the mess.

Anne followed the line of torches more quickly than ever this time. She arrived at the mouth of the cave and strode past her hanging clothes to walk naked and unthinking out into the rain. The droplets were fat and warm, and Anne spread her arms wide and her legs slightly to let the wet clean downpour wash over her. The warm wetness pleasantly pounded against her bare skin, washing away the sweat and the blood and the last lingering remnants of her strange paralyzed dream.

The falling raindrops felt like a million tiny hands scrubbing her clean, and Anne moved through warm sheets of it with fluid graceful mindlessness. From the outside it may have looked like she was dancing to a drunken rhythmless beat, or stalking a flitting faerie through the rain; within she was a river that snaked and flowed through the warm valleys of her own body. She could not tell where the water ended and she began, and it felt as though as many thrumming droplets permeated her skin as beaded up on it. Her slow movements opened every curve and crevasse to the rain, and for a long time she swam graceful slow strokes through the falling stream.

CHAPTER 12

She wasn't going anywhere any time soon. After her long liquid dance, still naked, Anne tiptoed out to the road. She couldn't tell if it was morning or noon; or perhaps the dim light came from a full moon. The road was lost behind sheets of rain, and Anne knew the windshield would show her the same impenetrable translucence no matter how fast the wipers moved. Somehow she was relieved to have the decision made for her, and Anne stopped at the rental for a banana and a bottle of water. The rain still came down, and the outside of the bottle was as wet as the inside as she stepped into the tunnel.

Anne shook the bottle and the fruit, feeling warm droplets of water splash across her naked skin. By the time she made it back to the room of fire, the banana peel was in one hand and the empty bottle was in the other. She set them both down just inside the entry, kneeling momentarily while her eyes stayed on the center of the room. The torch she had thrust in the sand was still there, still burning, and it cast an eerie glow over the corpse. Dancing flames moved flickering light across the skull, and for a moment Anne thought she saw flesh and hair. The dark hollows became dark eyes, and the dead grin looked for a moment like a sweet living smile.

She stepped towards it, and it was a skull again. Long

shadows stretched out behind the body, dancing on the sand in a way that was dreamily reminiscent of the way Anne had just danced in the rain. As she came close, Anne knelt and peered more closely at the remains. There was a thin strip of leather wound around the corpse's neck, and Anne hooked it carefully with her index finger to pull it toward her. The brittle length ended at a leather pouch that tugged at the collar of her cloak before leaping forth. Anne lifted the leather over the skull and worried at the opening of the pouch until it revealed its contents.

It looked like salt, a small mound of dry white crystals at the bottom of the mostly empty pouch. Anne set it near the book where it lay open on the sand and moved unhesitating toward one of the unexplored passages. She was full of a strange electric energy still, her body alive in a way that made her mind not want to think. Later, she could struggle with the backward script to see if Clare Anne's story was worth reading. Right now she was going to follow her feet where they took her, walking naked through the mysterious passages and leaving the occasional droplet of blood between her bare footprints.

Maybe it was the light breakfast, or the long warm sleep, or the thrill of new discovery. Anne spent the whole day walking through the endless caverns, sometimes running along a passage she had already traversed. When she ran, the flame of her torch streamed behind her; the faster she ran, the longer the trail of light. Nude and unafraid, Anne ran for miles, delighting in her bouncing breasts and the long trailing flame. She came to several collapsed tunnels, and a couple of dead ends that looked like they should have gone on further or connected to something. Mostly the tunnels were all bare rock overhead and soft sand underfoot, and Anne was happily exhausted by the time she found her way back to the circle of fire.

The torches all still burned, and Anne gave up trying to puzzle out how they did. Grateful for the heat and the sparing light, she curled up in the sand and rested her hot cheek on the cool pages once more.

CHAPTER 14

It was impossible to tell what time it was in the circle of fire, at any time of day. Anne came awake and watched the drifting remnants of an already forgotten dream flit away to burn in the flames. She sensed there was something important about the dream; but looking back at the fleeting images, she saw nothing other than the usual steamy scenes. Dismissing the thought, she went a little ways down one of the other two passages to answer the more urgent call of nature. Her purse was at the other entrance, and her tissue supply was getting low anyhow, so Anne let herself drip dry as she made her way to the center of the circle again.

She'd go out in a little while, to see if the rain had stopped and to take another natural shower if it hadn't. Right now Anne wanted to read more of the mysterious message that someone had written backwards in blood on the strange pages of the ancient book. Dragging the open relic carefully toward the light of her planted torch, Anne moved her eyes closer to the fragile open pages. Her eyes went wider as she realized that she could read it; the strange jumble of characters were the same, but somehow her mind was transposing them into words as she read them. She went back to the first page.

"You are a bright and curious woman," Anne read aloud. "Yet there is a fire that burns within you brighter and hotter than your curiosity. The flames of your desire are frightening to you. You fear that if you give in to them you will be consumed by them. Yet you must allow them to consume you if you are ever to be free."

Anne lifted her eyes from the page. Looking into the light of her torch, she saw her own naked kneeling form somehow in the flickering flames. She watched herself stand tall and proud and confident in her mind, her fears all burning away in the searing heat. She felt a slow smile pull at the corners of her mouth as she turned her eyes to the book once more.

"You must meet the demon of your desire," she read quietly. "You must meet your demon and you must overcome your fear of it. If you can embrace your demon in every way, you will be grateful for it your whole long life. If you cannot, your troubles will be many and your years will be few. Turn the page now, that you may meet your demon."

Slamming the book shut, Anne stood up straight in the sand. For a moment she had a stark moment of clarity, and the voice of reason in her head stepped forth from the silence that had swallowed it. Anne saw herself as she usually did, from a critical outside perspective. What was she doing? Why was she still naked? Was she aware of how silly she looked, her nude body covered in her own dried sweat and blood?

Then her hunger or her thirst or her desire swept the voice aside, and that primal silent awareness took over once more. Anne glanced down at the book where she had left it. She could read the cover now too; and somehow she knew that it was the bloody fingerprint she had left on it that made the words swim into focus.

"The Book of Desire," she read aloud, then looked at the finer print underneath the bold lines.

"Manchester Edition." There it was, another familiar name that did nothing but deepen the mystery. Anne knelt in the sand, opened the cover. She read the first page again, this time wondering if the words were maybe not just meant for her. Did they change every time a different person's blood invoked their magic, or did the book really only fall into the hands of hungry women like her? Were there really more like her out there, buffeted about each day by winds of want while bubbling just beneath the surface with the constant boiling burn of desire?

Her heart pounding, Anne turned the page. Part of her expected a monster to leap forth from the glassy surface, but it was more shifting characters taking shape before her eyes. She read aloud again.

"The first thing you must do is protect yourself and the world from the demon. Draw a shape on the floor in an unbroken line. It can be any shape, so long as the unbroken line meets itself before ending. This will create a space in which the demon can be contained. Draw the shape with a natural substance such as ground herbs, chalk, gypsum or salt."

Anne paused and rose in one fluid motion. She plucked the torch from the sand and approached the bag of salt she had removed from the corpse. Stepping across the sand, she noticed a distinct line of stark white woven into the light gray in the sand at her feet. Holding the torch higher, she traced the line until it turned sharply, then traced that line to its next turn. After she had mapped out two of the points, Anne realized she was following the pattern of a five-pointed star drawn in salt in the sand. Stepping back, she saw that a wide circle had been drawn around that. The circle took up most of the room, the long lines of the pentagram just touching its wide circumference. The pentagon within the center was the space she had been sleeping in, sweating in and dreaming in.

The pouch was mostly empty, and the salt had to be kneaded within it so it wouldn't fall out in chunks. Anne wound her way around the circle, letting a thin stream of salt pour continuously from the pouch as she bent over the sand. She was amazed when she met her own beginning with just enough salt remaining to cover the first few inches over again.

It seemed like it might be an ancient coming of age ritual, or some symbolic steps to help her find some new level of self-control. Anne didn't particularly like the demon symbology, but she understood it well enough. She had forgotten the entries that had puzzled her earlier, and her decision to read the backward entry word by word today.

A part of her expected the next step would be drinking some magic potion, or eating some unavailable root or leaf. She wasn't about to go searching around in the pouring rain for a psychedelic plant, no matter how detailed the book's description of it or how good the trip promised to be. Drawing a line in the sand was where she drew a line in the sand; no more hocus-pocus.

The next instructions were surprisingly simple. Anne read them out loud in the bright warm light of the blazing torch.

"Stand or sit in the center of the symbol," she read. "Place the book on the ground before you, open to the first blank page. Close your eyes and state your desire as clearly as you can. Picture what you desire in your mind while you give voice to it. Let your thoughts become feelings, and let those feelings grow until every part of you becomes excited with your desire. Leave a part of you behind when you are finished, and go away from the book and the symbol to cleanse yourself. Cleanse your whole self, with water and then wind and then the heat of a flame. Then return to the book."

Well, as long as it was still raining and gusting wind, Anne could do all that. Most of it she was going to do anyway, eventually. Why not here and now? Placing the book perfectly within the center of both the pentagon and the circle, Anne stood over it for a long moment before she turned the page.

Her hesitation was not fear, or anxiety, but because she had caught a glimpse of the stretching tendons of her feet and the flexing tautness of her calves. Anne's eyes watched the flickering shadows dancing across her skin, felt the warmth of the fire meet the heat of her desire as it began to pour from her in soft silent waves. Naked, flushing, uninhibited and unafraid, Anne bent and turned the page. The next was full of strange symbols, not yet translated by her blood. After the pages of foreign words and the backward story was another page of unfamiliar words. The next page was blank, and she left it open there.

CHAPTER 15

At first it was all in her imagination. After one last look at the book, and at the blank page she had opened it to, Anne closed her eyes and thought of all the things that she wanted. She could feel them somehow as she thought of them, sweet kisses on her cheeks and lips, a tender touch taking her hand. It wasn't long before she began to imagine the kisses lingering, then straying to her breasts; and it wasn't long after that before she began to touch herself.

The touches were light and loving at first, like the kisses and touches she was imagining. Her own hands brushed back her hair, stroked her belly and traced light slow lines under her breasts. Anne thought of Henry, of all the times she had imagined them together. His face came to her easily behind her eyes, swimming into focus with that sad sorry look he always gave her now. She let his face fade as she licked her lips and cupped her breasts, tasting her own sweat and feeling her nipples start to stiffen.

Another face came into focus, the face of the boy at the coffee shop. He was smiling, and not looking sorry for it at all. Anne thought of kissing him, of touching him, of letting him touch her. She felt her own hands on her body while she thought of his, touching her belly and breasts and hips with fingers that sought to explore every contour with tender urgency. Anne's heart began to pound in her chest as she thought of his kisses trailing down her bare breasts and belly.

Words tried to form on her lips while her hands and her thoughts continued to move seductively in whatever direction they chose. She felt her light loving touch over her most intimate folds, watched one face morph into another again behind her eyes. Now it was the young man from the airplane kissing her, touching her, smiling at her. He was so handsome, his kisses so soft and wet and enticing on her flesh. Anne lowered herself to her knees in the sand and moved her thighs apart to let her hand between them. Her other hand kneaded one breast, and then the other, while she rubbed at the rising flesh around her wet warm opening.

Her thoughts spun in whirling circles like her fingers, her inner storm building in the mounting heat. As his head dipped down to move between her thighs, the face changed again. Now it was the dark older Mexican man she had seen at breakfast, looking up at her and smiling before licking and kissing her where she was pressing forward into him. Anne let her thighs part even more under the curious questing movements, and felt his tongue move to taste her more deeply. She heard him moan, like he had just taken a bite of his favorite food, and felt the tickling tingling of his tongue vibrating with the sound.

A part of her was still trying to think of just what she wanted, exactly what it was that would satisfy her hunger enough to sate it. In the privacy of her mind, she wondered while she touched herself. With the dark smiling face lapping at her in a way that made Anne feel an impending inner explosion, she thought of what she had come here for. In her most inner thoughts, the ones too private to even record in her journal, she had planned this vacation the way only someone living a life steeped in fantasy could.

She had hoped for two or three lovers on this trip, maybe one that looked enough like Henry to make her never want him again. If she was going to be honest with herself, Anne wanted to return to California with as much sexual experience as she felt like she should have had by now. It seemed like every girl in high school had been with at least one or two guys by graduation, besides her and Raina. Even Raina had Henry, and everyone thought it was so adorable that they were waiting until their wedding night.

At the thought of him, Henry's face was the one with his mouth on her now. He looked up at her in her mind while Anne's fingers caressed her soft fleshy folds, and the words she was looking for formed suddenly in her mind.

"I want to lose my virginity to Henry, like it should have been," she said quietly. His mouth was moving in her mind, stoking her rising heat with his swirling tongue.

"I only want him for a night, though," Anne continued, as his mouth or her fingers gave rise to a network of pleasant tingles all over her naked skin. "Then I want someone else, someone more experienced but not too experienced. Someone gentle and caring that doesn't have a whole lot of hangups about sex. Then maybe someone a little older, a man who has been a man for long enough to show me something more about being a woman."

Anne's fingers were moving faster, and she dropped forward onto one hand while the other coaxed the deep rising tide within her to new heights. Flush with the effort and her own pleasure, Anne felt her heart pounding in her chest. She lowered her naked breasts into the sand, spreading her legs further and rolling her finger across the nexus of her pleasure with more intensity. With the weight of her upper body pressing her breasts into the soft scratchy sand, Anne reached back to grasp one buttock firmly. She felt herself open up just a little more with the movement, enough to feel the warm air of the fiery space heat the inferno within her even further.

"I want to be confident in my sexuality," Anne whispered, her breath coming faster and hotter. "I want to be comfortable in my own skin."

The pleasure took her then, pounding her from all sides and from within at the same time. She looked to see what face was licking and kissing her into pleasurable oblivion. It was a kaleidoscope of shifting features behind her eyes, and Anne collapsed into the sand under the crashing waves of ecstasy. In her mind he moved, spreading her legs and bringing his body close to her. It felt so real when he plunged inside of her that Anne wondered if she had accidentally slipped one of her fingers into her own deep wet heat. She hadn't; and once she realized it, she let the fantasy have its wonderful way with her.

Writhing on the ground, feeling the touch on her skin and the urgent hardness within her, Anne touched herself until the series of explosive climaxes faded to a pleasant tingle all over her body. For some time after she lay there, spent on her back in the sand, her arms and legs spread wide. One hand stretched out to touch the book where it lie open, the hand that had touched her breasts and her body while the other burned between her legs. The wet and bloody hand that had taken her through the doorway of her desire lay in the sand, tiny granules sticking to the streaks of warm fluids. She felt the heat from the ring of fire and her nearby torch, on her flushed skin and between her legs.

Remembering the words from the book, Anne rolled toward it slowly. Holding it in place with one hand, she smeared the slick bloody fingers of the other across the page. The smooth textured blankness of the page began to whirl into a spinning vortex as she pulled her hand away. Anne didn't notice the movement, nor did she see the stain fade into the pattern. She was already on her feet, headed toward the cleansing.

With each step she took she felt more energized, more enlivened. By the time she stepped from the ring of fire she was almost running, caught up in the happy movements of her own body. Each time she lifted her leg to step, the motion was accompanied by a lift in her spirits. Each time her foot landed in the sand, a pleasant shockwave burst through her body. Her movements were something between a child's unworried and unhurried skipping and a wanton woman's seductive dance.

She burst from the mouth of the cave minutes later and planted her feet in the muddied ground underfoot. The rain was a pleasant warm sprinkle at first, and Anne spread her arms wide and threw her head back to let sheets of it wash over her. Then a gust of wind caught her up in it, and she tottered in place while it buffeted her body. Anne worked her toes, feeling her feet sink into the mud as she did. The wind rocked her back and forth in place, and the rain went from a steady sprinkle to a hot wet downpour. Clenching the mud with her feet, Anne let the rest of her body sway in the gusting wind and the pounding rain.

Every part of her could feel it, as the wind blew itself and the rain in every direction to splash against her skin. For a few seconds she couldn't even breathe, as water and wind climbed up her nose and down her throat. Then she coughed, and sneezed, and her lungs filled up with something more magical than air or water.

Anne pulled one foot from the mud, holding it aloft to watch the falling rain wash it clean. Even the wind was there, tickling the bottom of her foot and flowing between her toes. The wind and the rain were her lovers, touching every part of her and leaving it feeling wet and warm and profoundly refreshed. Anne felt the wind's intimate caress as she lifted the other foot, the rain following with steady rhythmic sheets of cleansing pleasure. She stood like that for a few wonderful seconds after all the mud had dripped from her foot, letting the waves wash over her pleasantly.

Then she was back in the cave, dripping rain. Each drop seemed to carry a fear that it had pulled from her depths with it, and her countless anxieties exploded on the sand alongside the falling droplets. Anne plucked a burning torch from the wall and walked to the next three where they sat dark and dormant affixed to stone. Taking them down one by one, Anne worked each handle into the sand and lit each torch. Soon she stood in the center of a smaller ring of fire, there in the wide passageway. She let heat pour from the flames into her body, drying her clean naked flesh.

Moving with the slow sway of a timeless dance, Anne let her arms and legs drift with the random flickers of the shifting flames. She felt the heat on her skin, in her hair, drying her and cleansing her in a way that she had never experienced. The fire seemed to be on the surface of her skin, soaking into her cells to open them and burn away the lifetime of tense wanting clenched tight in each tiny part of her. Its heat probed at her more intimately than the wind or rain had; Anne seemed to be breathing in the warmth from above and below. She watched from within as the rising heat met the falling heat within her to pleasantly burn away the last clinging remnants of her tense anxiousness.

By the time Anne was done bathing in the hot wash of the crackling flames, she felt like a different person. The trembling girl that had walked into this cave a day or two ago paced her as a wispy ghost for a few steps down the passageway. Watching the woman that Anne had become moving confidently away from her, the ghost burst into a million pieces of fading light that drifted forgotten to the sand.

CHAPTER 16

Anne made her way slowly down the passageway. She felt the soft prickles of every grain of sand under her feet, the wafting warmth from each of the lighted torches that lined the path. She felt the muscles of her legs as they moved and flexed, the smooth naked skin stretching and relaxing with each measured step. There was an ease to her gait that was as unfamiliar to her as the confident way she was holding herself. Though strange, the posture and the walk felt as natural to her as her nudity.

Her mind did not race down the path ahead of her, thinking forward to what she might do next or back to what she had done there last. Thoughts did not swirl about her head in a disorienting whirlwind of confusion, or fill it with stabbing judgements. All of her attention was on her own movements and the scintillating textures of flames and space and sand. Her body seemed to glide along the passage, her steps as quiet and thoughtless as her mind. A new sensation rushed through her, an open hollow happiness that enlivened every cell of her body with the rushing heat that flowed through the hollow.

The heat from the torches seeped into her skin as she passed them, and her heart began pounding despite her easy stride. Anne felt her naked skin begin to flush with hunger, and for the first time there was no guilt or shame or fear in her building desire. The still warm air moved against the mounting heat as she walked, and hot tendrils sent a network of tingling sensations through her body.

She didn't touch herself, but not because she was ashamed or afraid to; the warm air against her nude form was already seducing her, the hard sharp softness of the sand was touching her lovingly. The entire arch of the cavern seemed to be embracing her as she travelled its sandy trail. Desire was all around her, and within her, and she swam easily through the thick waves of it as she neared the room with the book and the hot ring of fire.

Pausing before the entrance, Anne saw the carefully folded pile of clothes she had stepped out of so long ago. Next to the pile was her purse, and the remnants of what little food and drink she had taken in while she had been here. She stared at the strangely unfamiliar items for a long quiet moment, looking out of her new eyes at the old castoffs. Then a noise came from within the room, a scuffled step that stood out against the crackling sound of flames. It sounded more deliberate than purposeful, as if whatever lie within the circle of fire was making the noise to alert her of its presence more than to actually move about.

Fearlessly, Anne approached the entrance. She stood in the arched doorway, making her eyes take in the unbroken circle before letting them go to the shadowed form in the center. There was no longer any question of whether or not she believed in magic; she *was* magic. Anne could feel the tingling on her skin and in her cells, the same inexplicable power that was the source of the unending flame pouring from the torches. There was nothing to wonder about, or explain; there was only Henry, standing in the middle of the room and watching her looking at him.

"Hello, Henry." Anne took two steps toward him. His eyes were on her nakedness, and his lips wore a slight frown.

"Hello, Anne." Henry was wearing clothes, his usual jeans and pocket tee and sneakers. She could see the outline of his muscles through the thin fabric of the shirt.

"What are you doing here?" She knew the answer to the question, but Anne wanted to hear it from his lips.

"I…I am here to take your virginity, and…and to give you mine." Henry had always been uncomfortable with the subject of sex. It was the one complaint Raina had about him when Anne let the topic come up. Even his gaze looked unwilling as his eyes travelled over Anne's nude body. It was as if her nakedness was a magnet that kept drawing them to her, despite his obvious desire to look away.

Anne had a new confidence about her, and she didn't rush in with thoughts of how maybe her boobs were too small or her butt was too big or maybe he just didn't find her attractive. Instead she watched his nervousness, a small smile forming on her moist lips.

"Do you plan to do it with your clothes on?" Anne looked him up and down, her eyes smiling more than her mouth.

She watched him undress, watched the familiar parts of him come into view and then the unfamiliar. Anne had touched it, once, but she had never seen it. Henry didn't seem as uncomfortable with his own nakedness, although it revealed that he was clearly not aroused by hers. Still his eyes were drawn to her somehow, and he reached out his hand tentatively to her.

Careful to step over the line of salt, Anne entered the circle. A hot wave washed over her as she did, and a sheet of fiery red blinded her for a moment; then she was taking his hand and holding it to her chest. She knew he could feel the pounding drum of her heart, feel the hot rushing blood under her skin. She wanted him. He was Henry; she had always wanted him. She wanted to taste his kisses and feel his touch.

He didn't resist her as she stepped into him, but his arms were slow to encircle her. Anne raised herself on her tiptoes, lifting her lips to his. It all came rushing back to her as she felt the soft yielding flesh of his mouth. His lips were as unresponsive as his dangling lack of desire, though they were both pressed against her hot naked skin. With her arms about his shoulders, Anne lowered herself to her flat feet and looked up at him curiously.

"You don't want me," she said. It wasn't an accusation. It was actually a huge relief, because the realization brought another along with it.

"You don't like girls," she said, more quietly.

Suddenly it all made sense, as she saw the last few years of her life from a different perspective. Henry hadn't grown distant because her parents had died; he had drifted away from her because her sexual advances were becoming too much for him. The one time she had touched him had been at the drive-in. Henry had gotten his dad's pickup for the night, and Anne had secretly been hoping that Henry was secretly hoping that tonight was the night. Even if they didn't go all the way, she knew they would be rounding some bases.

When she had started kissing him, Henry had been distracted like he always seemed to be. When she lifted his shirt and started touching his belly and his chest, he had stiffened. Taking the wrong cue from his arched back and drawn in belly, Anne had plunged her hand down his pants. She had encountered a handful of soft confusion; and she had pulled her hand back to her chest in shock at her own action as well as his lack of reaction. They had sat through the rest of the movie in uncomfortable silence, talked about the show on the way home a little, then he had dropped her off.

The next day he had broken up with her. Not long after, not long enough after, he had started seeing Raina. Anne's parents had been gone for months, and she was starting to get her life back together when Henry broke up with her. It had sent her into a downward spiral of self-criticism, and every other boy had been another possible rejection that she couldn't bear. So she looked out of every alluring pair of eyes through her own filter, judging herself and casting herself aside before they could. Like Henry had.

Anne fought the urge to laugh as she watched him shake his head. She realized what a burden this was for him in the same moment that her own burden lifted. Then she thought of Raina, and felt a twinge of pain for her best friend. A part of her tried to wish it wasn't true, that this Henry and her conclusion were both figments of her imagination; but Anne was done with weaving illusions. She had no judgement for Henry, and she even understood why he hadn't said anything.

Still shaking his head, Henry moved into her and brought his face down to hers. The touch of his lips on hers sent all of her thoughts skittering in a million different directions, and the taste of his tongue brought back something deeper than memories. They had shared their first kiss together, a quick peck, when they were just children. Through all of the years that followed, until he had paired up with Raina, they had explored the innocent pleasure of the kiss together. His mouth was the only one she had ever actually tasted, and the flavor stirred the depths of her desire.

Henry's kisses were the same as before. Anne had never thought to examine the tenderness or the tentative way that his lips moved against hers. She did now, but only for a moment. Henry had been trying to convince others, and perhaps even himself, that he liked girls. His kisses had been musky fuel for the fire that burned within her, and Anne had taken them eagerly without ever thinking of how hard they were for him to give.

Now he was trying to prove his desire to her, and she could feel the strained effort of his mouth on her lips and his hands on her body. She tried to move away, to explain to him that it was okay, that she understood. Henry wouldn't let her lips leave his, and he clutched her tighter to him as he felt her try to back up. Anne let a few thoughts in, wondering if this was real; and if it was real, was this actually Henry? How could he actually be here? And if it wasn't really him, why imagine him this way? Even if Henry didn't like girls in real life, he had always wanted Anne in her fantasies. How strange was it for her to fantasize him being hesitant with her, and afraid of himself?

Anne let the thoughts fade as Henry began to kiss her neck. The tickling tingling touch of his lips became an explosion of heat as his lips lingered at her shoulder. His hands moved to cup her buttocks, and squeeze them gently, and Anne dismissed her mind altogether. If Henry wanted to prove that he was straight by having sex with her, Anne wasn't going to stand in his way. She let the feel of his touch and the wet of his kisses overwhelm her, and felt her mind become as slippery as her moist neck had become under his mouth. This was no time for thinking.

One of his hands moved to where her buttocks came together, and Anne felt his fingers move between her legs as she parted them slightly. His touch was tentative and gentle, and his feathery caresses were pleasurable in their innocence. They tickled the rising flesh around her heated folds, and she felt the response so close to his hand. She moved into his fingers, and soon they were wet and slippery and touching her where she wanted them to.

Anne moved her hand between them, reaching to touch

him like he was touching her. His other hand was already there, kneading his own flesh into some response. It was working, too, and she felt him growing as she grasped him. Henry let his hand move away, to touch her tentatively on her hip. Anne kept one hand on his slowly stiffening flesh while she guided his hand with the other. Taking it from her hip, she put his hand on the smooth rounded curve of her buttock. Putting her fingers over his, she squeezed his hand like she wanted him to squeeze her bottom. Firm but still tentative, Henry squeezed. Anne felt herself open up further to his other hand, and she pressed her hot wet center harder into its moving fingers.

She gasped with her pleasure, and began working the flesh in her hand more aggressively. Clenching and stroking, she leaned back in Henry's arms to feel more of her weight press into his hand. One of his slick digits slipped inside of her, and Anne felt another pleasured gasp escape her lips. She was ready; she had been ready ever since that night at the drive-in. She had wanted Henry inside of her then just as she wanted him inside of her now, just as she had wanted it in all the moments in between.

She was ready; Henry was about halfway there. Anne pulled away, but only for long enough to lower herself to her knees in the sand. She took him in her mouth inexpertly, still holding most of him in her hand. She looked up while she worked her tongue in circles around the mouthful of flesh, searching his face for clues as to what he might be enjoying about what she was doing or what he might have her do next.

Henry's eyes were closed, and Anne didn't give a thought to what her fantasy might be fantasizing about. The part of him she could taste and feel was growing harder and bigger in her hand and her mouth, and soon it was standing up on its own. Anne took Henry's hand then, and pulled him down on top of her in the sand. He descended awkwardly, opening his eyes long enough to position himself just as awkwardly, then bumped his hardness against her even more awkwardly.

Reaching down, Anne grasped him and moved him into her. Already he was not as hard as before; but Anne felt him come back when he slipped inside of her, and closed his eyes again. He moved against her, and inside of her, and the tentative thrusting motions were pleasurable enough. She watched his face for a moment, then looked over his chest and his arms. Henry's face looked as strained as his muscles, and taut lines stood out across both. He was inside of her, and all of the way, but there was no urgency or tenderness or eye contact; he was just there.

When he cried out, Anne was relieved. She made sure she was smiling up at him when he opened his eyes. Henry looked amazed that he had finished, and relieved that it was over. He smiled back at her, taut worry lines creasing his face once more.

"Was that…was that okay?" He flushed, only the second time she had seen it.

"That was wonderful," Anne lied, kindly.

She moved away from him.

"There will probably be blood," she reminded him. "It was my first time, and I'm having my period. I'll go get cleaned up and bring back something to help you get cleaned up too."

He was already on his feet, looking down at his bloody limpness and fingers. He didn't look disgusted by it, but he didn't look particularly pleased by it either. Anne stood up and moved toward him, kissing his lips lightly one more time.

"Sorry," she said, out of courtesy rather than shame.

"It's okay." He smiled weakly.

She turned and made her way toward the edge of the circle. With one bare foot inside the salt shape and the other outside of it, she paused and looked back over her naked shoulder.

Henry was looking down at himself, his muscled torso flexing in the torchlight with his efforts to not touch himself where her touch or her fluids lingered. The kindest thing she could think to say came to mind, so she said it to him.

"Hey, you big stud," she smiled. "You just popped my cherry."

Henry stood up taller, and brightened visibly.

Anne turned away and lifted her other foot over the salt. She strode up the passageway, thinking of Henry and Raina and the tremendous weight that had been lifted from her. It was still pouring down warm rain outside, so she stood in it with her arms spread open wide. Hot salted tears sprung from her eyes, sadness for her friends and relief for herself; but they were washed away in the fat falling droplets that burst warm and wet against her face. The last clear thought she had before the rain washed them all away was that there was not much reason for her to think of Henry anymore. Or ever again.

CHAPTER 17

The rain felt good on her skin, and the quiet felt good to her mind, but Anne remembered what she had said after a few minutes. She went to the rental to get her last two bottles of water, then brought them back down the passageway with her. She hoped Henry wouldn't need more than one of them to clean up; she was thirsty. Her skin had been drinking in more water than her lips, and her nude form glowed in the firelight with the moisture that had soaked into it.

When she arrived at the circle, Anne was both relieved and unsurprised to find it empty. She checked to make sure the line was unbroken, following the wide circle with a careful eye, but she knew it was. Henry was gone, and she was glad. Trying to kiss him or touch him or make love to him again would have been awkward discomfort for both of them. The book was still there, open in the sand, and the corpse still lounged nearby; but Henry was gone.

Anne knelt by her clothes, setting down one of the bottles of water. As she stood and uncapped the other, a movement caught her eye. She turned, the open bottle in one hand and the cap in the other. Squinting, she saw shifting shadows take a solid shape, and in the next moment someone else was there. She capped the plastic bottle and let in fall at her naked feet in the sand.

It was the boy from her last day in Maysville, her last lunch with Raina. He was as naked as she was, a little taller than her but not by much. His slim frame was not ripply or muscly like Henry's, but it was attractive in its own way. It felt different when she crossed the line to move against him, like she was close to him in a way that Henry's sinewed chest had not allowed.

He wanted her, it was clear the moment their eyes met. When she touched him he touched her back; it was not the tentative hesitant touch she had just felt, nor was it the perfect loving tenderness of her fantasies. It was the groping grasping hands of a young man as overcome with desire as her, and apparently as inexperienced at it. His hands wanted to touch her everywhere, and she let them, as a new flavor filled her mouth and his unfamiliar scent filled her nose. She couldn't describe the difference between Henry's musky odor and his earthy smell, and she didn't have to. She let the smell of him fill her lungs as she breathed him in deeply. She let the taste of his tongue fill her mouth, and she let his sweet kisses feed her fire.

When he kept his hands still somewhere, she moved into his touch seeking the pleasure. When he groped her awkwardly, or poked at her painfully, she focused on the pleasure of his kisses and his earthy scent. He wanted her so bad, she could feel the evidence of it throbbing between them. Anne put her hand on it, and it stiffened further at her touch. His kisses grew as desperate as his touches, his tongue thrusting in her mouth like his flesh was thrusting in her grasp.

Anne stepped back from him, keeping her hand on the part of him that wanted her the most. She smiled while he reached for her, let his hands brush her breasts and then fall on her shoulders.

"James," she said, remembering. "My name is Anne.

It's very nice to meet you. Will you put this inside me?"

It seemed a funny exchange, her holding him like she was shaking his hand and introducing herself. It wasn't his hand in hers, however; and neither of them laughed.

"Hello Anne," he breathed. "It's nice to meet you too."

She lowered herself to the sand and spread her legs as he moved between them.

"Be gentle," she murmured. "I haven't done this much."

He nodded, as if to echo the sentiment, but he didn't say anything. Anne was glad she had spoken up; his eyes were glazed over with hunger, and all of his remaining attention seemed dedicated to approaching her slowly. His fingers touched her first, all around her wet center and then a little inside of it. The first part of his rigid desire pushed at her slick edges; and then it was inside of her. He held himself there, not moving, so Anne started to rock her hips lightly against him. She felt the part of him that was inside of her move around; she felt the hot flush of want; she felt his throbbing need.

She felt something else too: he was bigger than Henry had been down there; not painfully so, but in a way that was probing more insistently at her insides. He was only inside of her about halfway now, and she felt filled up like she hadn't before. It was adding ecstatic mild shockwaves to the rising tide of her hunger, and she thrust against him to swallow him whole. They both gasped, together; and then their mouths were one and their bodies were one and they moved in unhurried desperation against one another.

They found a sweet rhythm, and his entire rigid length moved nearly all the way inside of her and nearly all the way out again over and over. Each time it was covered in more of her slick mounting pleasure, and her mouth was filled with more of his tongue and his taste. She breathed him deeply into her while she took him deeply into her, and the mild shockwaves began to build into a sweet spiraling tension. It was different than the tension she built when she touched herself, and the only relief for it was in the thrusting length of his hardness.

Their mouths were joined above as their desires intertwined below. Anne had her eyes closed, awash in his taste and his touch and the building waves of her pleasured tension. It was as if she was winding herself tightly around him, clutching him to her with her mouth and her hands and her hunger. She opened her eyes to look at him for a moment. Anne watched his face, so handsome and so close as he kissed her. His eyes were closed too, and he had a sublime look of pleasure; she could feel his smile in his kisses and see it on his face. He was swept away by the deep plunging rhythm of their intimacy and the wash of his own set of sensations.

Anne wondered what it felt like for him as she closed her eyes to be swept away right along with him. She felt his movements against her, and inside of her, while she returned his kisses and felt his fevered thrusts. She felt how much of her was him, how a part of her had a part of him held firm in her slick hot grasp. The part of him inside of her was not an invader, or an intruder; it was a perfectly fitted puzzle piece that had been placed right where it belonged. As she felt his hard length find its perfect place over and over, Anne felt the deep swell rise to a peak within her.

She squeezed around him without thinking of it, trying to forestall the warm wet wave for a few more moments of open acceptance. Her clench caused an immediate response in both of them: he got even bigger, his thrusting more insistent; and Anne was immediately awash in the climax she had been trying to stave off. His engorged length was hard like stone now, and she swam around in her ecstatic waves under him. Anne felt like a puppet being moved about by someone's arm inside of her, smiling and twitching and coming as he worked her from within.

Then he tensed, and a hot splash of wet filled her up even more inside. He kept moving, and she kept coming, and soon the hot splash and her own slick fluids were one warm wet cocktail all over him and inside of her. He hovered over her, holding his weight with his hands in the sand on either side of her. Looking down, still inside of her, still moving slightly down there in the most delightful way, he kissed her forehead.

"You can lay on top of me," she smiled, still pulsing around him. "I won't break."

He settled on top of her, all at once, and Anne thought for a moment that maybe she might break. Then she shifted, and her arms and legs were around him while her face was right under his. She felt delightfully smothered by his body, clenched tight around a warm heavy blanket that was returning her hugs and kisses. He stopped moving, except to kiss her, but he kept the whole length of him inside of her. Anne felt it grow softer, slowly, felt the waves of her own raging pleasure subsiding.

Tender, smiling, he kissed her cheeks. Then he brushed his lips across hers, and spoke. His voice was as soft and tender as his kisses.

"That was amazing," he breathed.

Anne kissed him back. She nodded, smiling.

"Was that okay for you?" He frowned a little.

"Oh my gosh! Are you serious?" Anne giggled, kissed him again. "That was amazing for me too! Didn't you feel me?"

"Everything I felt from the moment I first touched you was a little overwhelming," he admitted, flushing. "Being inside of you was a lot overwhelming. I couldn't feel anything but wonderful the whole time we were making love."

Anne hugged him tighter, kissed him more deeply.

They lay like that for awhile, talking and kissing, circling the subject of their coming together like their kisses circled each other's faces. At some point she felt him getting hard again, and she giggled again, and the combination sent fresh waves of want through her body. They made love once more, with less urgency and more lingering passion, coaxing longer and deeper pleasure from their bodies. The ecstatically extended effort had them both sweating and gasping for breath, until Anne turned him over and rode his rigid flesh to another shared explosive climax. She lay in his arms after, her bottom pressed against his slick front, and slept soundly in the circle of his embrace.

CHAPTER 18

When she woke up, Anne was alone again. Her head was resting on the open book, although she didn't remember laying it there, and she felt renewed and refreshed like never before. She left the circle of salt carefully, fire flashing behind her eyes as she did. Dropping to her knees in the sand, she unscrewed the cap from the bottle of water she had discarded in her hunger and emptied it in one long drink.

The falling rain outside did not mystify her any more than the eternal burn of the torches inside the cave. Nor did it surprise her, and she bathed in in gratefully yet again. Her muscles and her insides were a little sore, but it was an invigorating soreness that cried out for more pleasured activity. Even the rain seduced her, washing away the soreness and cleansing her with wet warm tickling tendrils.

Halfway up the tunnel she was dry from the fires that lit the passageway. The warmth began to soak into her naked skin once more, and her hurried movements coaxed the heat into every crease and fold. By the time she saw the lighted entrance ahead, Anne was ready for what she hoped lie beyond. Her face was flush, her shoulders thrown back confidently, and her nipples stood out in their stark sensitivity. A thin sheen of sweat covered her slim body, and she could see the reflected light of the flames dancing over her hungry curves as she stepped through the archway.

"Todd," she remembered aloud. He smiled at the sound of his own name. Anne returned the smile. He was as nude as her, tall with a stout sinewy build. He was so handsome.

"I'm sorry for not introducing myself to you before," she said, her shyness a thing of the past. "You were so forward, and so good looking, you kind of got me all flummoxed."

"Sorry," he said, not sounding sorry at all. "I know what I want."

"And what is that?" Anne smiled at him over the salted line.

"First," he shrugged, "to know your name."

Anne giggled; she still hadn't told him, had she?

"Anne," she said, stepping up to the line but not crossing it.

He smiled, repeated it. "Anne. It's nice to meet you."

She liked the way he said her name; it sounded like he wanted her.

"What else do you want?" she breathed.

"I want to kiss you," he smiled. "I want to touch you everywhere, and feel your body close to mine."

Anne's hand went to her heart as it began to pound harder in her chest. Her eyes wide, she leaned over the line to hear his next words.

"I want to know what it feels like to be inside of you, and what it sounds like when you come." He opened his arms to her.

She could see that he was already anticipating the feeling as much as she was. The first thing she touched after carefully stepping over the salt was the part of him rising towards her. Anne cradled the length of him in her hand as she stepped into his arms, lifting it so it was captured between them and pressed against her on one side. She felt it throb against her belly while he brushed strands of hair back from her face, and the first touch of his lips on hers was tender innocence by comparison.

He kissed her once, then again, then he tasted her lips ever so slightly. Anne opened her mouth, covering his with her wet eagerness, and he smiled as his tongue lightly flicked against hers. His hands were on her body, tracing the smooth lines of her back and her hips. His touch was tantalizing sweetness, gently exploring her contours with carefully curious fingers. Anne found herself moving into his touch, not to put his hands where she wanted but to show him how much she was enjoying where they were. His fingers were like warm magnets, pulling her into his touch and soaking his heat into her skin.

Anne tangled her fingers in his hair, anchoring herself by wrapping her arms about his neck so she could better fall into his touches. She pulled his lips close to hers again and again, filling her mouth with the taste of his. It felt like his flavored kisses were the food she had not eaten, and she swallowed them to the very depths of her hunger. Rather than sate her or placate her, the sustenance of his taste only sparked her need for more. Anne kissed him passionately and deeply until they were both gasping for air. His hands were cupping her breasts, and her nipples were throbbing with a painful pleasure, when he lowered himself to the sand.

His hand trailed from where it had been lingering lovingly under her breast, down her arm to grasp her hand. It was the only place he was still touching her, and she ached from head to toe for his nearness, so she let him pull her gently to the ground next to her. Instead of climbing on top of her, or pressing himself insistently into her, he knelt by her side and kissed her while his hands trailed lovingly over her breasts and belly and neck. Anne's body was still aching for him; and the ache was coming from deep inside of her now, where she wanted him to be.

Lying on her back, Anne's desire blossomed under his tasty kisses and trailing touch. She felt her legs start to spread while the lines his fingers were tracing over her heaving ribcage moved high enough to tease her nipples and low enough to tease the pleasant throb of her aching need. Anne felt her flesh rising to meet his touch as it moved; her breasts, then her belly, then her hips. His hand finally moved between her legs, while his flavor filled her mouth, and she moaned while his tongue and finger slipped inside of her. Anne felt her thighs parting even more, the only part of her not leaning hungrily into him, and she felt him move between her legs at last.

He didn't stab at her, or hesitate; instead he put himself right up against her, gripping his own hardness in his hand while pressing it into the soft hot flesh rising around her folds. Then he was in her, just a little, still describing slow circles that pressed pleasantly against her inner ridges. His hand moved then, away from his own flesh to touch her all around where he was inside of her. He moved deeper into her, still rolling his hips to the rhythm of her pounding heart, and his hands trailed around her hips to cup her buttocks.

Gripping her firmly for the first time, he still moved circles inside of her. Anne felt herself opening up to him as his hands squeezed her and spread her in the most wonderful way. He worked his hardness in a slow narrowing spiral inside of her, kissing her while massaging her both inside and out. Her legs were in the air above him, one trembling and pointing straight up while the other was bent to rest and rub against him. It wasn't until she saw her leg pointed to the heavens, trembling, that she realized her whole body was shaking as well. His slow spiraled movements within her were ushering her quickly towards a gasping and trembling climax.

Anne wrapped her arms and legs about him as the shaking turned into a low pounding hum that buzzed in her every cell. Her whole body was vibrating in place, clutching him inside and out. The spiral inside of her was where the hum was most intense, and Anne held herself in place against him so that he could move just as he meant to. The buzz was in her ears, and in her chest, and in her hot wet clenching hunger. He seemed to know what she could feel in her own trembling depths, that the end of his slow spiral was the beginning of her climactic dance.

Little by little, he moved deeper inside of her with that tingling and tantalizing swirl of pleasure. He kissed her, and she tasted him, and with every taste and every touch she invited his everything more deeply into her. Anne hung from his lips like she hung from their junction, open and trusting of his touch and his taste and his sweet spiral. When his lips left hers, it was only for a moment; just long enough to move his mouth to her ear and whisper his desire to her. His breath was on her neck when his words found her ear, and they both sent the hum that buzzed through her body to a high pounding pitch. Anne's cells danced at the sound of his voice.

"Come for me," he breathed, hot on her neck. "Come for me, Anne."

Then he moved all of the way into her, and her body was awash in the raging flames of her climax. Anne's arms and legs were still around him, and she clutched him to her while she let his movements splash the heat about inside of her. Even now he was moving perfectly, describing deep circles in her while the length of his hardness massaged the depth of her wetness. Her orgasm was cresting to a new height, and his mouth on her neck and shoulder was driving her pleasantly mad with tickled ecstasy.

Anne was crying out without realizing it, a pleasured wordless encouragement that rose and fell in pitch as he whirled delightfully within her. Even when his mouth found hers again, her moan travelled muffled through his body to layer another tingling vibration to his hard swirl. She couldn't believe how hot she was, how wet she was, and how every part of her seemed to be singing the pleasure she felt in her molten core. Her orgasm seemed to stretch far and wide, and it lasted so long that she felt like she might drown forever in it.

After awhile she came back to herself within the cacophony of delight dancing around in her body and bursting forth from her mouth into his. She let him out of her embrace, intending to lay him on his back and ride him in that same swirling manner. Instead he turned her over, gently but firmly grasping her hips and rolling her. Anne felt the hard countless granules tickle her nipples and her cheek, as she crossed her arms over each other in the sand over her head. His hands lifted her hips, and Anne felt him inside of her again as she got her knees under her.

Her throbbing heat had cooled as they moved, but Anne realized that she had only been on pleasant pause. The slick hard heat of him inside of her had her heart pounding and her cells singing like before. Now he was insistent, and his thrusts were long and hard and penetrating, and she welcomed it. She wanted to feel his pleasure gushing inside of her along with her own, and she thrilled at the way his urgency pressed her forward again and again. Then he grabbed her buttocks as he had before, only from behind, and began to knead and massage them in his grasp. Anne felt him deeper inside of her than ever, and harder, and thoughts of his pleasure or her own were washed away in her sudden swim in a sea of ecstasy.

Anne heard her own voice, muffled against the sand,

laughing or crying or some sound of abandon that was a combination of both. She felt him so deep in her, felt the pleasant rubbing touch of his hands spreading her, and at last she felt him grow even bigger inside of her. The hot wet splash made her cry out one last time, and she backed up into him. She was a warm full wonderful mixed mess of them inside, and she ground her hips into him so his length would stir their stewed shared pleasure.

He went soft almost right away, and he slipped easily out of her to collapse beside her in the sand. His muscled chest heaved with his exertion, and his body gleamed with sweat in the torchlight. He was smiling, and glowing a little. Anne felt a warm glow emanating from her own skin. She lay facing him and scooted herself closer in the sand. Her sand-covered breasts pressed against his chest as her legs entwined playfully in his. Anne leaned forward, without thinking, and licked at the sweat on his chest. It tasted of him, of her, of their sex and of his essence; it tasted delicious, and she swallowed the taste to her satiated core.

Their faces inches apart, their bodies covered in sweat and sand, they smiled at each other.

"You are so beautiful," he murmured.

Anne smiled. "Thank you."

It didn't hit her until after she had done it: Anne had just accepted a compliment. She hadn't brushed it aside, or flushed and turned away, or waved it off with her hand; she had accepted it. She had let something that she had always fended off touch her, only to find the simple contact surprisingly wonderful. She kissed him.

"Your lips taste like heaven, or home," she breathed.

He smiled and kissed her back, moving his arm so they might both lay their heads on it. Their noses almost touching, their breath drifting from one open mouth to the other, they fell asleep in the crackling torchlight.

CHAPTER 19

Anne woke up smiling, alone again. She lay there for awhile, one hand flat on the indentation his body had left in the sand. The memories of last night flashed scenes through her mind, and it wasn't long before she felt the nearby flames tickle her naked flesh. She let it caress her from all sides, turning and opening her legs to feel the warmth climb inside of her. Anne didn't know how long she lay there letting the heat seduce her. By the time she lifted herself from the sand to seek the cleansing rain outside, she was aching to be loved and touched and lost in pleasure once more.

The torchlight held close to her as she walked, embracing and touching her until she burst from its glow to stand under the stormy sky. The droplets of warm water on her face and her breasts and her upturned hands were another layer added to her seduction. Teasing her and cleansing her, the wet rivulets that moved between her breasts ran a hot trickling trail down her belly to wash over her throbbing mound. She felt the water everywhere that she could feel, soaking into her skin and washing over the folds of her hungry flesh.

Then it was torchlight again, swirling its heat and its light around her and through her as she walked. Anne was dry halfway down the passageway, but she was dripping with desire by the time she reached the stone archway. She didn't pause before going through, or before crossing the line; instead she walked right up to the waiting young man and took his hand in hers. She smiled at the way his fingers held hers, tentative but wanting. Naked like she was, he was just a little taller than her. His smooth slim torso was covered in dark soft skin that she longed to touch and taste.

"I saw you by the pool the other day," she breathed, taking his other hand. "You looked so sexy, I went into my room and touched myself thinking about you."

He smiled, and squeezed her hand in uncertain response.

"I'm Anne," she continued, unperturbed. "What's your name?"

He flushed, and stammered, then smiled uneasily.

"Juan," he answered. "My name is Juan."

He had a thick accent, as she should have expected. His eyes were as uncertain as his voice, trying to look at her and trying not to at the same time. The only clear response her smiling lips and her touch on his hands were getting was the one she most wanted to see. He was getting hard, being that close to her, and his dangling desire slowly stood to attention as she watched. Anne smiled, still holding his hands in hers.

Leaning in, she brushed his lips with hers without quite touching the part of him growing towards her. His mouth was soft and shy, and he stood there unmoving while she left a trail of kisses down his chest and belly. She felt him trembling slightly under her lips: in shyness, anticipation or both. Anne lowered herself to her knees in front of him, pressing her soft cheek into his hard throb. Still holding his hands, she turned her head slowly to lick a wet path along his entire length. She felt the trembling of his body moving him against her moist lips and trailing tongue. Then she took him in her mouth and let her tongue move slow slick spirals around the curved end of his hardness.

He gasped, his hands clenching hers. Anne smiled and sucked, drawing him further into her mouth. The flavor of his flesh tickled her tongue in the most delightful way, and she sucked and licked him like he was a delicious spiced ice cream cone. She moved one of his hands to her hair, and felt his fingers tangle lightly in her dark thick mane. Letting her hand drift to his upright desire, she grabbed the length of him like a helpful handle and worked the hard rounded end of him eagerly with her mouth. His stiff stance and silly smile were all the encouragement she needed as she glanced upward.

Anne closed her eyes to taste her treat fully. She licked and sucked and swallowed the flavor of him until he began to whimper helplessly.

"Por favor…" he breathed. "Anne, por favor…"

She smiled around his pulsing hardness again. She liked the way he said her name. She liked the way he said please. She pulled him down beside her with both hands, one in his hand and one on his throbbing need. He was shy still, but eager enough; he lay on his back and lifted his head to see what she would do. One of his hands was still in hers; the other propped his head forward to watch her as she straddled him. When she lifted him upright and swallowed the first part of him into her hunger, his eyes went wide and a shudder went through his body. Anne felt it in his hand and in his hardness, and she sighed as she lowered herself onto him.

It was pleasant sweetness inside of her, like the tentative lingering touch of his hand in hers. He lay still, the only signs of his pleasure the wide-eyed look of wonder on his face and the sweet squeeze of his hand. And his hardness. The part of him that was inside of her throbbed in the most wonderful way as she began rolling her hips against his. Anne stoked her own fire with her movements, and the tide of desire within her rose in response. Warm wet waves of pleasure began to wash over her, as her cells sang sweetly to her of her impending climax.

Anne leaned forward, to press herself more effectively backwards into the place where their bodies were one. Her breasts flattened against his chest, and her lips tasted his mouth for a moment. Another wave washed over her, hotter and wetter, as her lips found his. Her tongue moved inside of his mouth, and she tasted that same spiced flavor that had filled her mouth before. She began to lift herself slowly to the end of his throb, then lower herself fully onto him again. Anne felt the ebb and flow of herself being penetrated pleasantly over and over again, and the primal need within her made her start racing more rapidly towards her ecstatic ending.

She was bucking her hips and rolling them at the same time, watching his head loll in the sand with pleasure, when the first wave hit her. She cried out, bucking harder against him and tasting his neck with her open mewling mouth. His climax hit her from within, wet and hot, and another crushing wave of pleasure washed over her. He was still hard, so she kept riding him and her own warm drenching waves of orgasm. Out of the corner of her rocking eye she saw him, his eyes rolled back in his head while a silly unconscious smile lit his face.

He went soft ever so slowly, and she moved slower against him. For the longest time she rolled him around inside of her. It felt like she was slowly drifting from a cloud high, her swirl of consciousness stepping from its misty edge to float effortlessly back into her flushed sweaty body. Her slow roll came to rest at last, with his flesh and his wet splash still inside of her. Anne looked down, saw him smiling and felt him squeeze her hand. She lay on top of him for awhile, her weight slippery with sweat on his chest and his flesh slick with her satisfaction inside of her.

When she moved her weight off of him, he rolled over and yawned. Anne smiled and brushed his thick dark hair back from his face. His eyes drooped sleepily, and she continued to trace her fingers lightly across his brow until his satisfied smile became a low rumbling snore. She watched him sleep for awhile, then roused herself and made her way once more up the long sandy path. The rain poured over her, and into her, and she was glad when she returned to the ring of fire that it was empty.

She ate what little food she had remaining, and sipped at her last bottle of water. Anne wasn't ravenously hungry, or thirsty, although she should have been. She felt as though she had been consuming her partners' passions, digesting the string of sensual experiences. The glow of her skin and the spring in her step made her wonder if this was a sustenance more meaningful to her than food.

CHAPTER 20

Somehow Anne sensed that her time in this magical place was coming to a close. A part of her was happy for it; she was a different person now, a different woman. She wanted to walk back into her old world wearing this new skin, and look with fresh eyes at her former life. Anne got the sense that everything was going to change for her soon, and the part of her that was looking forward to that change itched for tomorrow.

There was another part of her as well. It was not sad at her change, or to see this impossible and special adventure end; it was more of a happy melancholy, a desire to have one last look back at who she used to be before leaving her old self behind forever. Like a snake slipping free of a layer of skin that has grown too tight, or a butterfly winging free of its chrysalis, Anne wanted a final glance over her shoulder at the life that had both confined her and defined her until a few days ago.

She walked the network of dark tunnels that wandered all over under the earth. She went outside, and hiked in the forest around the rental car. The rain seemed to be pounding harder than ever, and the wind whipped her wet hair delightedly against her fire-kissed face and breasts and shoulders. The moist ground was soft and yielding under her bare feet. It seemed as though she was as much a part of these woods as the ring of fire was a part of her memories. Every leaf and rock and raindrop were an extension of her, and she was an expression of each of them.

In her delighted exploring, she stepped free at last of any regrets from all of her yesterdays. Anne left every last bit of who she used to be in the wet woods and dark tunnels, leaving her worries to melt in the puddles of rain and shadows. At some point she found herself alone with her journal, trying to read the old entries. It was someone else's words, someone else's fantasies, and she felt both invasive and disinterested trying to follow along. She thought of burning it, for a moment, or trying to write in it; but what could she say? How could she put into words the transformation that had taken place in her? She had left the journal and the thoughts behind to wander again in the rain and the woods.

Naked, wet and warm, Anne felt something shift inside of her as she stood under the falling droplets. The ring of fire was calling to her one last time. She let the magnetic pull build within her until her feet refused to stay still any longer. The forest floor touched and tickled their bare bottoms as she walked, and the rain trickled over her shoulders and breasts and hips. The wind buffeted her in intimate bursts, sending warm wet kisses between her legs as they shifted. It felt like she was cleaner than she had been before, no matter how deeply the wind and rain had previously penetrated her. It was a moment of silent wondering before she realized that the minor aches and stiffness that she had been habitually ignoring had finally passed. She was past the bloody and painful part of her cycle, and felt renewed and refreshed having gone through it.

Anne hesitated before entering the cave. She didn't just sense that it would be her last time stepping through the obscured opening; she knew it. Her dwindling supply of food and water had dwindled to nothing today; she had to go back, weather permitting or not. There was no concern or worry surrounding the certainty; somehow Anne knew that she would get out of here safe, and back to Maysville. After that, everything that used to be her life would surely change.

Brushing the mossy curtain aside, Anne stepped into the cave. The warm glow of the first torches washed over her, and the shadows of her own curves in their light was captivating seduction to her eyes. She watched her own naked thighs shift and swing as she walked, watched her breasts bounce with her steps. She felt the palms of her hands tingling with the thought of touching, and every inch of her naked skin longing to be touched. The tickling rough softness of sand underfoot and the teasing tendrils of heat from the torches seduced her silently, while that magnetic pull drew her deeper into the cave.

Her anticipation was building like never before, even more than with Henry. She didn't stop at the line of salt out of shyness, or fear; instead she stood there for a moment to steady herself, as the hum of hungry excitement reached a resounding climactic pitch within her. Their eyes met over the line, and her desire saw its own reflection in his dark steady gaze. It was the handsome man from her last full meal, the older man who had smiled at her in the most open and friendly manner. He was smiling now, but the smile was different. It was intimate, it was inviting; it was a smile more full of promise than any smile she had seen before. It was a smile that was just for her, and just for this moment. Anne couldn't help but flush a little as she smiled back.

"Hola," he said. "Yo te amo Francisco."

Anne's smile fell a little, and her nutrient-starved brain

took a moment to translate. *Hello,* she thought to herself. *I am called Francisco.*

She saw his eyes on her body, and she felt her smile widen once more.

Hello Francisco, she thought silently, looking for the words that would convey the message to him. *I am Anne. I'm sorry. My Spanish is no good.*

"Hola Francisco," she murmured, smiling. "Soy Anne. Lo siento. Mi español es no bueno."

He chuckled, and the effect was magical. His dark eyes crinkled at the corners, the muscles of his slim abdomen stood out in lines, and the long hanging part of him shook between his legs. He was handsome in a calm and thoughtful kind of way, and his happy calm demeanor crystallized in his easy laugh. His hands were relaxed at his sides while he chuckled, though his eyes were open invitations to her every desire.

"You're beautiful," Anne breathed. She let her eyes drift downward. "And big."

"No entiendo," he said; although he chuckled again and glanced down, following her gaze. He seemed to understand exactly what she was saying. He seemed to know exactly what she was wanting. His eyes travelled her body as hungrily as hers trailed over his. He reached out his hand to her, and Anne crossed the sand between them in three easy strides. She moved close to him, and felt his touch on her shoulders as her arms encircled his waist. It seemed natural to embrace him, to feel the length of his body along hers. They were almost the same height; all she had to do was tilt back her head to taste his lips as he kissed her.

His body was both pressed against her and relaxed into her. His hands were gentle sweet caresses on her cheeks, and soft soothing brushes in her hair. There was no insistency to his touch or his kisses. She felt like a fine sculpture being lovingly examined by the artist one last time before hardening into unbreakable stone. His lips brushed hers a dozen times, and her flushing cheeks, before he slipped his tongue between them to taste hers. Her desire was to open her mouth and taste his flavor fervently, but Anne let his light loving touches and slow lingering kisses set the pace. Her lips parted gradually under his tender treatment, blossoming with wet like the folds between her legs. When his tongue touched hers at last, Anne felt like the penetration was as intimate and as exciting as the one she was beginning to burn for. His flavor filled her mouth, and he tasted of ecstasy.

Now she did open her mouth to him completely, covering his lips with hers. That was not a comforting taste, or a familiar flavor; the way his mouth tasted on hers was explosive, and dramatic, and irresistible. She thought of the sleek predator in the wild, catching the scent of its favorite prey on the wind. She thought of her pheromones, and his, and how they seemed divinely designed to fire off a deep and rapid series of responses within both of them. She thought of how it felt to have her own rising tide of desire crash into his, and how sublime it was to feel as though she had met her match in so many delicious ways. Then she became all of those things, gave in to all of those things, and lost herself in his embrace.

When his hands moved to her body, his mouth moved to her neck. He tasted the droplets of sweat that had beaded on her shoulder as surely as she felt his mouth hungry on her flesh, and they both pressed more closely into the contact. Anne felt his loving touch rove over the curve of her back and buttocks, and every sweet lingering touch felt her moving into it. She couldn't get close enough to him, or feel his touch in enough hungry places, and she was glad when he pulled her down into the sand.

Gently guiding her with those careful loving hands, he laid her back and lifted her arms over her head. He intertwined her fingers in the sand, then trailed his touch along both of her arms ever so slowly. His eyes were ahead of his touch, though they kept going back to it. Anne felt like a precious discovery, or a beloved creation, under his fingers and his gaze. One hand paused at her face, brushing strands of hair away to adoringly trace the soft lines of her cheekbones. The other hand was over her heart, around her breasts and belly. As it moved, she moved with it, rising into his touch to feel it more fully. Her heart was pounding harder each time his hand passed over her heaving chest.

He turned, kneeling, and let both hands drift downward while his lips moved to her chest. He kissed her over her pounding heart, wetting his face with the hot sheen of sweat on her breasts as he cupped them to press them to his cheeks. Anne thought of reaching her hands down to grab handfuls of his thick dark hair and press his head insistently downward. She was aflame, burning with the way she reacted to his touch and his taste. She could feel her own desire starting to form hot wet droplets between her legs. Her blossoming folds ached to feel the way it felt when he tasted her.

Resisting the urge to grab him, Anne let her fingers tangle in her own hair as she spread her legs wide and arched her back against him. His hand slid down the curve of her belly first, followed by his mouth. Then one hand was on her inner thigh, his thumb reaching to massage the rising flesh around her folds. The other hand was on her breasts, touching her hardened nipples at last, and his face was finally between her legs. He was just over the hot wet junction of her thighs, and she could feel his breath as he moved closer. He licked around her first, pulling her apart with his tongue on one side and his thumb on the other. Then he crawled over the sand to position himself between her legs.

For that short moment of transition, they were not in physical contact. Anne lay in the sand with her legs spread and her back arched, her fingers tangled in her own long dark tresses. She realized in that moment that she was on the brink of climax already. The way he tasted and touched had driven her pleasantly mad, and her entire body was pulsing with the need to dive into that hot sea and swim in it. When the moment was over, his hands were on her again: touching her thighs and her knees and her calves, then grasping her ankles and bending her knees to her chest.

Anne looked up, and saw the hunger in his eyes. She looked down, and saw it mirrored in his huge hardness. He was looking at her eyes and her face, at her breasts and her belly, at her bent legs and her wet blossom. It all seemed to be precisely enough to be exactly too much for him; Anne felt herself quivering with the same delicious feeling. Then he moved to taste her, and they moaned in time with the exquisite contact. His hands moved just as slowly over her breasts and belly; but the touches were more firm, and they coaxed a deeper pleasure from her flesh. It was all she could do to fight off the explosive climax that threatened to pleasantly wash her away.

She felt like she was holding a thin creaky door against the full weight of a flooding sea of endless wet. Anne knew why she pressed so hard against it, why she was exhausting her will to resist it. She wanted to feel every nuance of his lingering touch, to sense the subtle certain pleasure in the way he handled her. She felt precious and tender and sensitive under his hands and his mouth, and she wanted to wait a few more trembling moments before she exploded apart into a thousand ecstatic pieces.

His hands were cupping her buttocks now, his thumbs laid out to frame where his mouth was licking her lightly. He squeezed his hands, pressing his fingers into her flesh and his thumbs into the throbbing mounds around his tongue. Anne felt herself open up to him, as his digits worked to knead her flesh and the rising tide pounded at the door within her. Then his whole mouth was on her, and she was being sucked pleasantly out of herself, and the door within her burst to splintered pieces all around inside of her. Anne was moaning, and crying out, and he was moving down there like he was only getting started.

It felt like he had flipped up some control panel within her, and was pushing her buttons perfectly with his tongue and his thumbs. Anne's legs were akimbo, her toes pointed straight out and away from her body as she spread her legs as wide as she could for him. She was trembling, and whimpering ecstatically; and still he circled her final explosive button teasingly with his tongue. When that warm wet touch found her secret center at last, another wave of climax washed over her. She rode the wave like he rode her button, and soon her ecstatic whimpers became pleasured cries.

Thick wet smears of her drenched his face, and waves of orgasm rocked her body; still he wasn't done down there. One of his fingers moved inside of her, and he bent it up and towards himself. Anne felt the tide rise further, higher than she knew it could, as she pressed that part of her fervently into that part of him. His finger moved, beckoning her to a higher plateau of pleasure. His tongue licked while his mouth sucked, and Anne was somehow surfing the tsunami as it rode her inner ocean from one shore to the other. Every time it crashed against her shore, she cried out with the explosion; then she was riding another giant wave, the wind and wet washing away everything but her trembling anticipation of the next wondrous crash.

By the time he moved inside of her she was dripping wet, and he was rock hard. He worked the edges of her opening while he covered her lips in her own thick flavor, slipping his tongue in her open mouth and sinking his desire deep into hers in the same sweet moment. His movements were still deliberate, and delicious, as he slid his full hard length into and out of her again and again and again. He was stirring a stew whose ingredients were all of the wanting she had for him, and his eyes looked as awash in pleasure as Anne felt when he looked at her between kisses. Her hot wet flavor was all over his face, and in her primal ecstatic state she began to lick the thick taste of herself from his lips and the wet salted sweat from his chest.

He began to move fervently against her, sliding along her body on the slick heat between them. Anne felt as though a dam had broken within her, and that she would somehow have to live the rest of her life riding the thunderous waves of this interminable climax. Then she was overcome by the need to taste him, and to taste herself on him, and she sat up to push him back into the sand.

She positioned herself to drip into his mouth as she took his throbbing hardness into hers, and she felt his tongue tasting her again. Anne sucked and licked, moving her mouth on him like he had been moving himself inside of her, taking that big throbbing mixture of them as deep into her hunger as she could again and again. Then her hunger grew to thirst, and she sucked as hard as she could until she felt him grow impossibly big and fill her mouth with flesh and fluid. They both found their way down her open throat as she sucked him deeply into her until she needed to breathe.

His prolonged cry of pleasure was music to her ears, and

it echoed through her body to wash her away in another wave of orgasm. Anne rolled off him, away from him in the sand. She stood, her breasts heaving and gleaming with sweat. He moved towards her, reaching out for her; but she stepped away. She could still feel the waves pounding at her shores, the wet hot droplets trailing down her inner thighs.

"I have to go," she breathed, although she took a half-step back towards him when she said it.

He shook his head, either not understanding or not agreeing. Still sitting in the sand, he reached out to her. Anne cast a long look over her naked shoulder, at the passageway that would lead her away from here forever. The she took another step towards him and lowered herself into his open arms. His touch brought the tingling electric pleasure to her skin once more, his lips filled her mouth with their tastes coming together again, and Anne let herself begin to drown in the sea of their shared desire one more time.

CHAPTER 21

It was no longer raining outside. Of course; Anne had to consider that every warm wet droplet had been in her mind. She had to consider that this had all been in her mind, a pleasant informative hallucination that had been real only in that it had been profoundly transformative. She had to consider these possibilities, because the possibility that the experience had been real was now too terrifying to consider. She looked back over her shoulder one last time as she sprinted up the tunnel, her clothes and purse clenched in a bundle to her chest. It was mostly dark; and empty, but for the torches and their light. Anne kept running.

Just as she was about to burst from the mouth of the cave, a voice cried out behind her.

"Anne!" It echoed along the stone walls, and they started to tremble.

She stopped, naked, and screamed back at it.

"Leave me alone!"

"Don't leave me here!" The voice boomed out, as dust and small rocks drifted to the sand. "You can't leave me here!"

Anne stood her ground long enough to scream one more time.

"Leave me alone!" Her words echoed back at her, and more falling debris filled the cave. She peered into the shadows, certain she could see a horned fanged monster with the body of a man but covered in thick red reptilian skin. He was loping through the shifting falling rocks and sand on black cloven hooves, his tail swishing along behind him. Then the falling pebbles and shifting sand became small rocks and heavy boulders, and she thought she saw him stumble. The debris drove her back, out into the open, and the tunnel collapsed with a thunderous rumble and a blast of hot air in her face.

She looked back, once, but there was nothing but another pile of rock that had gathered at the base of the high hill. It didn't even look fresh, nor was the ground under her feet even slightly moist. Anne leaned her face into the sun, and scanned the horizon. There was not a cloud in the sky.

Feeling a little foolish, but still changed, Anne unwound her clothes from her purse and put them on. She pulled the keys from her purse with a hand that only trembled a little as she did. The car started right up, and it was clear which direction she needed to go as soon as she pulled onto the road. Anne was feeling more confident, and less foolish, as she passed the town where she had last eaten an actual meal. Her stomach grumbled, and her mind went to last night.

"Adios, Francisco," she murmured under her breath as she pulled onto the highway that would take her back to the hotel. She knew where she was going now, and she tossed the unmanageable mess that was her map into the tiny back seat. Her eyes went to the passenger seat.

Anne screamed.

The book was there, sitting on the seat as though she had placed it carefully next to her purse. But she hadn't; she had tried to get away from Francisco after they had made love again, and he had tried to stop her. They had struggled, and she had seen his features change as they tussled in the sand. His face had stretched and turned a deep mottled red, and short sharp black horns had sprouted from his forehead. His teeth had stretched to a row of sharpened biting teeth, and he had gnashed them at her as she had broken loose of his clawed grasp.

She had stumbled away from him, dragging her foot through the line of salt in her hastened efforts to escape him. He had thrown his entire weight at the air above the break, and his red scaled arm had clawed at her while the rest of him was pressed flat against some invisible barrier. Anne had grabbed her purse, wrapped her clothes about it while she ran, and only looked back when she was near the end of the tunnel.

Anne had left the book in the circle. There was no way it was sitting on the seat next to her, mocking her decision to call all of this a hallucination. After a moment's calm consideration, Anne worked the window crank. Hot air blasted her face as she scanned the rear view mirror, then swept her arm against the car after she had hurled the book into the thick vegetation along the highway. She glanced from the road to the passenger seat a dozen times over the next few miles, and somehow she wasn't surprised to see it there again the thirteenth time. She tossed it out again, and it reappeared again, and after awhile she just gave up.

It was still hot, and bright, when she got back to the hotel. Anne grabbed her purse and left the book on the front seat. She didn't lock the doors, hoping fervently that someone would see it and take it. In her room, she drank the bottle of water on the table as she let her clothes fall to the floor. She was not surprised at all to see the young man lounging by the pool when she stepped outside; somehow Anne had known he would be there. She strode along the pool, her shoulders back and her breasts forward and her fire-kissed skin gleaming in the sunlight. When she reached his side she stood over him, smiling.

"Hello, Juan," she breathed. "You are a very handsome young man. Would you like to come back to my room with me?"

He looked at her in confusion, either wondering how she knew his name or translating her words in his head into his own language. Anne didn't wait for a reply; she spun on her heel and walked away from him. She knew that her shifting buttocks were almost entirely bare in the red and white bikini, but she didn't mind; it was why she had chosen to walk away.

The lounge chair scraped against the poolside concrete as he rose behind her, and Anne saw her own smile reflected in the glass as she slid one pane aside. She left the door standing open and stopped halfway in the room to untie her top. It drifted to the floor as he stepped into the room, and her bottoms followed. She walked past him, naked, and slid the door into place behind him.

Anne walked a slow circle around him, trailing her fingers over his chest and his back. She stopped in front of him, nude, and ran her hands over his chest and down his belly. When they encountered his swim trunks, she hooked her thumbs in the waistband and pulled them down. As she lowered them to the floor, and coaxed his feet up and out of them, Anne felt him dangling hot against her face. She smiled up at him as she turned her head and took him in her mouth.

It was exactly as she remembered it, his spicy taste and his tentative touch as his hand drifted to her hair. Even the growing flesh in her mouth was a familiar shape and size, as familiar as his flavor. She pushed him back on the bed, and his eyes went wide as she put her mouth on him again. She sucked until he was moaning on her bed and throbbing in her mouth, pulling his flavor and his flesh into her throat with her hunger. She smiled around his hard pulsing throb, licking it one last time from base to tip before moving on top of him.

His hands were on her hips, gently resting in trembling uncertainty over her skin. She grasped him in her hand, positioned him where she wanted him, and put him inside of her. They both gasped; and his eyes rolled back in his head while she began to move her hips over him. Anne worked him around inside of her, pressing his rigid flesh against her yielding inner walls. She was up on her knees, straddling him and moving in swift swirling circles with her hips. She let herself down, little by little, until all of his hard flesh was inside of her and the swirl stirred her insides into a stormy wetness.

Anne's breath came faster, her breasts bounced as she rode him harder, and she looked down to see him watching her. His eyes were wide with wonder, and she knew she was beautiful and sexy and primal by the way she felt and by the look in their wide darkness. She felt her skin prickle, and a bead of sweat raced between her breasts; and then the room was lost in an explosion of light and color and the chorus of their pleasured moans. The hot wet part of her that had swallowed him whole was clenching him in a way that she couldn't control, and she felt like she was gushing liquid ecstasy all over him. She thought she was going to tremble and shake until she tumbled off of him and away from him for a moment; and then she felt him get bigger as she got hotter and wetter.

The warm splash hit her, and she bore down on his length. Grinding him into her, stirring their mixture, she grasped at the last fleeting glimpses of ecstasy as she collapsed on top of him.

That was real, Anne thought to herself, rolling off of

him. She looked at his stiff glistening flesh as it slowly softened. There was no blood. Of course; the cave and the book and the nights of passion had also been real, just as real as the cursed tome that waited for her in the rental car. She started to climb on top of him again when a loud series of knocks sounded at the door.

Anne crossed the room without thinking, throwing the door open nude and smiling. The man stood there a moment, aghast, then glanced past her.

"Juan!" he shouted. The next string of words were an angry garble to her, and she saw the young dark stranger pull on his trunks and slip out the sliding glass door. The man spoke clear english then, looking hard in her eyes as if allowing his gaze to drift south would burn his retinas.

"Miss Miller," he said. "Checkout was an hour ago. Will you be staying another night with us?"

His eyes did drift then, but it was to the door that Juan had just exited through. Without using words in either of their languages, he clearly indicated that she was not welcome another night.

"No," Anne shook her head. She smiled again. "Is it really Sunday?"

He nodded.

"Already?"

He nodded again; he was frowning now.

"No," she said again. "I have a flight to catch. I'll be out of here in five minutes."

CHAPTER 22

Anne would have left the book in the rental car if the attendant hadn't been right there and watching her. She had given up on leaving it by the roadside, but there was no way she was going to try to get it through customs. The looks and the questions would be too much. Every inch of space in her luggage was crammed full of something; she had made sure there was no room in any of her bags for the book to cleverly reappear in one of them. Clutching the tome to her chest with one hand, Anne dragged her suitcase with the other.

The first waste bin she saw with an opening large enough was right inside the airport. Anne didn't look around, or say a silly useless prayer; she walked right up to it and dumped the damned book at last. She watched for it on the flight home, but it had nowhere to show up other than her lap. Still she watched for it, and was beginning to think that she had gotten rid of it for good as she left the plane and filed through the customs line.

It wasn't until she had tossed her things in the back of her own car in the next airport parking lot that she saw it again. She settled in the driver's seat, and there it was next to her. Anne didn't scream, but she did begin to tremble as her hand hovered over the book. It seemed more real, now that she was back in California. This was not some strange and possibly magical rental car in some strange and possibly magical foreign land; this was her car, in her home state; and there was that accursed book.

She thought about what she should do with it all the way home. There would be no throwing it out the window along I-5; traffic and litter laws and experience told her that. For some reason she didn't want to go home with it; she didn't want her new life to start out weighted down by this ancient tome. Anne had the feeling that if she took the book home with her she would somehow never be rid of it.

So she drove around, passing through Maysville on the highway and taking it on through to Grassy Valley. She drove around the quaint little town until it began to get dark, and by the time she headed west again it was pitch black out. The moon and the stars seemed hesitant to rise in the sky, and the only light she could see were the stabbing beams of her own headlights and the flash of others as they passed her.

It was strange approaching the small town from the east. At first she watched for signs of life or lights on the horizon; then the empty highway and the dark night sky and the exhaustion of the week hit her all at once, and Anne nodded off. She was still going nearly fifty miles an hour when her little car jumped the curb and landed in the Maysville lake with a loud splash. There was no one around, and the steering wheel struck her just as she began to come awake. The blow drove her deeper into unconsciousness.

The water slowly filled up the car, as blood dripped from her broken nose to stain Anne's shirt. She stirred, but she never did wake up. Anne drowned quietly in her sleep with the ancient book beside her on the passenger's seat, less than a mile from home.

EPILOGUE

Anne was gone. It was almost too much for Raina to bear when they pulled her friend's body from the lake. Although her life looked picture perfect from the outside, inside Raina had been slowly falling apart for years. There was no way she could get married this summer; it would be too soon, and all Raina would be able to think about the whole time was that Anne wasn't there. Anne had always been there; how could she go on without her?

Henry had been only too happy to postpone the wedding date, but Raina had been too preoccupied with her grief to examine his eagerness. She knew there was something he was keeping from her, and she was pretty sure she knew what it was; but Raina had her own dark sexual secret that she dared not share. Who was she to judge?

In the weeks after Anne's death, Raina bonded with Anne's aunt over their shared grief. Raina helped Clare clean out the house, and all of its memories. She was glad to be there as Clare cried unspilt tears over the sister she had lost so many years ago, and she had heard stories of Anne's mother as a child and a young woman. Digging through old files in the basement, Clare had found an intricately documented family tree. She had spent long hours tracing through the tangled lines and piles of papers, and made a surprising discovery.

"We're related!" Clare cried as Raina stepped through the door one day.

Raina hugged her. "What do you mean?"

"My mother, Anne's grandmother, was cousins with your grandmother."

Clare beamed and swept her hand over the dining room table, indicating the piles of papers. Many were yellowed with age, and the few photographs were all black and white.

"It's all in there," Clare smiled.

"So Anne and I were cousins?"

"In a manner of speaking, yes." Clare shrugged. "You were second cousins, or third. I think. I'm not sure."

Raina's eyes filled with tears. "Is there any way I could start calling you my Aunt Clare, or would that be reaching too hard?"

"Aw, sweetie," Clare wrapped her arms around Raina's shoulders. "I would like that very much."

They cried more tears, happy tears of discovery and fresh tears of loss.

After awhile Clare grew very serious, and she looked Raina in the eye.

"Raina," she said. "I know this isn't the best timing; but I know now more than ever that anything can happen, and at any time. I would hate to have you discover it the way I did, after losing someone. I would hate to think that you might be angry with me for not telling you when I had the chance."

Raina leaned forward in her seat, half excited and half afraid.

"What, Aunt Clare?" They both smiled when she said it. "If you didn't tell me what?"

Clare sighed. "They found a couple of things in Anne's car that I didn't share with you. One was her journal. There are some things about you in there, but it's mostly about Henry."

Shaking her head, Clare sighed once more. "It's mostly fantasies she had about Henry. If you read it the wrong way, it would sound like real accounts of him cheating on you with her."

Clare paused again, and Raina interjected quietly.

"What if I read it the right way?" she asked.

"Then you would see her passion, and her angst, and how little it all actually had to do with Henry." Clare smiled. "You might see more of yourself in your cousin than you may have thought possible."

Clare flushed, and added, "I know I did."

"What was the other thing?"

Instead of answering, Clare stood and moved to the dining table. She pushed aside some yellowed papers, and lifted a book from where it had rested under them. She handed it to Raina.

"What is it?" Raina asked. The book felt heavy in her hands, and it looked older than anything she had ever seen. The leather cover had dried red droplets on it. "Is that blood?"

Clare nodded, solemn. "It's how you read it. Open it. I'll show you."

Publisher's Note

Marilyn Kahr came to us late last year with a compelling idea for a series of romance books, and a manuscript for the first one. She wanted to get it into ebook format, and she also wanted to be accessible to her readers without getting too public. Marilyn thought it would be fun to make the most intense chapter a bonus chapter. For those that noticed that there was no chapter thirteen in the ebook, she left an invitation to message her. At that point, she would send a personal message and the thirteenth chapter in response to the inquiry. We thought it was another great idea, and we agreed. Then she decided that she wanted to make the print version available, and we had to ask: what do we do with chapter thirteen?

After much discussion, everyone agreed that it should be included; but at the end of the book. That's the order it was meant to be read in, after all; and including it in the story in numerical order might make the reader think things are about to get pretty dark. Marilyn says it's a good example of how she plans to approach writing another series she has in mind; if you like it, there's even more to look forward to. If you prefer the tone of Anne's story, take heart. Marilyn has committed to another book by the end of 2016; and having read the first few chapters, we are more than curious to see where the story goes from here.

So here it is, Chapter Thirteen of The Book of Desire: Anne. Marilyn would like it to be reiterated at this point that she welcomes all comments about her book at MarilynKahr@gmail.com.

Thanks for reading!
Sudden Insight Publishing

CHAPTER 13

Anne woke with the hard cold page of the book pressing her cheek flat. She heard that heavy hot breath again, and she felt it on the back of her neck. A strong grip behind her had a handful of her hair, and was pulling her head to the side and smashing her face into the book at the same time. The grasp was not painful or unpleasant, and the tug on her hair sent as many delightful tingles down her spine as the warm breath on her neck.

This time she could move, and Anne rolled away from the strong grip and onto her back in the sand. Her eyes went wide as they met his. They were the color of flame, and they danced with the fire that colored them. He smiled, still holding the length of her hair, and she saw sharp biting teeth in his smile at the same time as she saw two dark pointed horns on his forehead. His skin was a deep mottled red, and it stretched taut over his muscular neck and torso.

Anne smiled. Why not? She had made love to all manner of men in her dreams; why not a demon? She rolled back towards him, pressing her back and buttocks into him while moving her head away to fully feel the tug of her hair in his hand. He breathed, heavy and hot, and it was the same breath that had covered her body and ignited her passion before. She felt it on her neck, on her back, and she shuddered as his hand came around to pull her shoulder back and press her breasts forward. His touch trailed down her shoulder, raking sharp claws lightly between her breasts to tickle her belly. Then his skin touched hers, the pads of his fingers coming to rest for a moment on her bare midriff, and Anne gasped with pleasured shock.

His skin was hot; not hot like hers, but hot. Anne arched her back to move her skin closer to his, and felt a tingling flush form under his hand as he placed it gently on her body. It burned, but only a little, and the pain was a hot fire that burned away her tension and her fears while setting every cell alight with desire. Anne turned into him, feeling his other hand go from her hair to grasp her shoulder as she did. The hot contact of both of his hands on her body completed some magical circuit, and suddenly Anne's whole body was warm and wet as she pressed her breasts against his hard chest.

Her lips found his, and they were as hot as his fingers. She opened her mouth to him to feel a warm wet tongue flick at hers playfully, hungrily. With the length of her body against him, Anne felt as though the flames of her desire and the fire of his touch had caused an inferno to burst forth between them. She was so hot, her body slick with sweat and her center slick with desire. Anne moved away from him, to look down and see if he was wanting her as much as she was wanting him.

Smiling, Anne moved her face to within an inch of his throbbing hardness. She could feel the heat from it, rolling off his dark red pulsing flesh as his hand tangled in her hair again. He wanted to feel her mouth on him, and she wanted to taste him. Anne flicked her tongue playfully over his veiny flesh, until an inhuman sound came from deep in his throat. Half snarl and half growl, the sound spoke his need better than words could.

Taking him in her mouth, exploring the contours of his

rigid flesh, Anne felt him harden even further. Moving the taste of him around in her mouth, she moved away to trail a wet string between them from her parted lips. Then she was on top of him, pushing his broad dark shoulders back into the sand and moving her legs to straddle him.

The demon grinned, showing her those sharp teeth again. He hadn't bitten her, or slashed her with his claws, though she had felt the sharp points graze her neck and her belly and her tongue. Anne thought for a moment that he could consume her like an animal, if he wanted to. It was her last clear thought before she consumed him, lowering herself slowly onto him as he held his throbbing flesh to point at her dripping desire. She watched him disappear inside her, felt the hot rapid pounding of his heart like that's where he kept it. Then he was gone, at least that part of him, sunk so deep inside her that it felt like it belonged to her more than it did to him.

Anne let all of her weight press down on him, on the place where they came together. She rolled her hips, slowly, her hands moving to his muscled chest before she collapsed her own torso onto his. Her hips still moved against his, grinding him deep into her as her breasts pressed flat against his chest. She kissed him hungrily, his neck and his shoulders and his jaw, pivoting joyously on the part of him that was all hers. Then he bent, and his lips were on hers again. Anne thrust her tongue into his mouth, and felt the jagged sharp edge of one of his teeth open a small painless incision.

Suddenly his mouth was full of her blood, and her mouth was full of his tongue. Somehow he grew even harder inside of her, and began moving his hips to the same pounding rhythm that she was moving hers. Anne gasped as the length of his hardness slid in and out of her, rolling around inside her to the dancing beat of her own primal song. She felt the heat pouring off of him, crashing against her skin as hot waves splashed over her throbbing center. Every part of her began to tingle with her growing heat and impending internal explosion.

Riding him, clutching him, Anne felt herself begin to writhe faster against his rough skin. In her urgency she moved her body away at the same time as him, and she felt that hot hard treasure slip out of her. Before she could rush to reposition her possession, he pushed her back into the sand and bent her knees to her breasts. Then he was inside her again; only he was deeper this time, and driving himself more insistently inside her. He grasped her ankles with his strong red hands, and the little bit that his claws dug into her skin caused her more pleasure than pain. Anne cried out as he slid the length of his hard heat in and out of her slick center once again, faster than before. He had her pinned in the most pleasant way, and all Anne had to do was lie back and let it come.

And then come it did. With his hot strong hands around her ankles and his hard throbbing passion inside of her, the rocking movement of his hips was faster and harder than ever as her body quivered on the brink of climax. Anne felt her back against the rough sand, sliding back and forth and bouncing about across it in time with his urgent thrusts. Like the taste of her own blood in her mouth and the pinpoints of pleasured pain at her ankles, the scratching hardness at her back only seemed to open her senses further to the pleasure he was pouring into her again and again. Her body tensed, her fingers digging into the sand at her side, and Anne threw her head back as the first warm gushing wave of orgasm washed over her.

Her fingers clenched at fistfuls of sand while the rest of her body went limp. Anne's legs and torso flopped about like a rag doll under his continued thrusts while one paralyzing wave of pleasure after another washed over her. She heard her own voice moaning, then laughing uncontrollably. Her laugh sounded like one long ecstatic moan punctuated by the rise and fall of her voice as her hot wet possession moved inside of her.

Slowly the ability to direct her limbs came back to her, even as warm waves of pleasure continued to wash over her. Anne let go the handfuls of sand to put one hand on his chest and the other on her own. Rocking back a little, feeling the deep twinge move inside her in another way as she did, Anne put her ankles on the demon's wide red shoulders. She saw the little spots of blood where his nails had been as he moved his hands to her breasts, and watched one tiny trail of red start to roll toward her knee.

Her head lolled to the side as she felt him filling her up once more, and the blood was forgotten. The waves of pleasure took on another dimension as his thrusts stroked at this new angle, and Anne's laugh rose in pitch and volume until every thrust was punctuated by a loud happy shriek. Still the wet hot waves of pleasure washed over her, and Anne grasped at him and herself until her wildly waving hands had scratched them both. Light but clear, a set of raised welts turned the skin on her belly bright with lines to match the dark raised lines on the demon's chest. Still he thrusted, and still her head rolled back and forth in the sand in time with her pleasured giggling shrieks.

Suddenly Anne was empty, her body still. All the heat that had been pouring off of him and into her moved away from her as he did, and Anne sat up to gaze almost accusingly at him. His eyes still burned with fire, and she stared at the only flame she could feel while she edged towards him in the sand. Her legs open to him still, she leaned forward to put one hand in the sand between her legs and the other on the throbbing hard hotness that belonged to her. He moved away, just out of reach, and Anne could only look from where the veiny treasure was now to where it had been a few moments ago. Her look was insistent, and still accusing, and the warm wet waves still lapped urgently at her inner shore.

For the first time, he spoke. His voice was hoarse, with desire or his demon nature or both, hoarse and low and gravelly. The question was as much a growl as it was words.

"Do you want it?" he asked. "Do you want it all?"

Anne nodded, quickly and repeatedly. She didn't know what he meant; hadn't she just had it all? Wasn't that the entire length of his pounding passion that she had just consumed over and over with her own desire? She was still nodding, but he wasn't moving any closer, so Anne spoke her desire.

"I want you," she breathed, her own voice hoarse and thick with it. "I want it all."

He moved so fast Anne felt a twinge of fear as his strong hands grasped her at her hip and shoulder. He turned her over, his touch impatient but still gentle, his claws pressing light pinpricks into her skin but not penetrating her flesh to draw blood. As her face and breasts gathered little rough grains of sand in the sweat that stood out on her skin, the demon grasped her hips and pulled them towards him. Just as Anne got her knees under her, she felt his hard slick passion fill her up from behind. Again, it felt different than before; and again, her body began to tremble with waves of pleasure.

Anne felt her face and breasts against the sand, felt pieces of it poking at her as she was driven into the ground with each of his pounding thrusts. She reached her arms out, crossing them over her head in the drifting grains. Her whole body rocked with the rhythmic penetration, and every cell was singing her ecstasy. The warm waves of pleasure became a hot sea of satisfaction under his thrusting movements, and Anne swam about in it languidly as he pounded her with abandon. Now he was the one making noise, each thrust punctuated by a deep throaty growl that sent a fresh tingle up her spine every time she heard it.

She felt his hands all over her, on her rounded bottom and her heaving ribcage and all over her back. Anne didn't realize for several long lustful moments that she was crying out as well, and louder than him. She heard her own voice as if from very far away, crying out her earlier answer like it was the secret words to the spell that kept her writhing in unending climax.

"I. want. it. all. I. want. it. all." Anne's husky cries came to her through the crushing waves of hot wet pleasure, the words punctuated by his desperate pounding thrusts. She didn't know that he would grow even bigger inside of her until he did, and suddenly Anne was filled with hot liquid lava. She screamed, the waves of pleasure washed away in a flood of agony, and she rolled over and away from him in the sand. She got her first good look at him since he had flipped her over, and she realized that his torso was covered in her blood. It dripped red from his claws, and it was smeared all over his face.

Anne looked down at herself, saw jagged deep sets of claw marks almost meeting just over the slight rise of her belly. Craning her neck to look behind her, she saw a lethal network of deep claw marks. Thick rivulets of blood coursed from every wound. Collapsing in the sand, burning on the inside and bleeding on the outside, Anne got one last long look at the demon. He was smiling, standing over her while Anne's life drained slowly into the sand. She closed her eyes and let the darkness take her.

About the author...

Marilyn Kahr was born and raised in a small town in Northern California. She currently lives outside of Sacramento with her longtime partner, their beloved pets, and a rich fantasy life. She welcomes all reader responses to her book at MarilynKahr@gmail.com.

A note from the publisher . . .

Thank you for reading this book. If you are interested in helping authors and readers find each other, please take a few minutes and leave a review.

The easiest and most helpful sites for book reviews are **Amazon** and **Goodreads**. Your opinion counts, and your effort is appreciated!

Thanks for reading!

Find more quality indie books at
www.suddeninsightpublishing.com